THE TORTURE GARDEN
OCTAVE MIRBEAU

(LE JARDIN DES SUPPLICES)

TRANSLATED FROM THE FRENCH BY ALVAH C. BESSIE

British Library Cataloguing-in-Publication Data
A catalogue record for this book is available from the
British Library

Biography of James De Mille

James De Mille was born on 23rd August 1833, in the city of Saint John, New Brunswick, the second largest of Canada's maritime provinces. He was a professor at Dalhousie University, Nova Scotia, but was better known as a writer specialising in popular fiction from the late 1860s through the 1870s. De Mille was the son of the merchant and ship-owner, Nathan De Mille and spent his early education at Horton Academy in Wolfville, before spending one year at Acadia University, also in Wolfville, Nova Scotia.

De Mille soon wished to experience life outside of his Canadian city however, and consequently travelled with his brother, Elisha Budd to Europe, spending half a year in England, France and Italy. On his return to North America, he attended Brown University, the third oldest institution of high education in New England, from which he obtained a Master of Arts degree during 1854. De Mille then married Anne Pryor, daughter of the president of Acadia University, John Pryor, and was there appointed professor of classics. He served there until 1865 when he accepted a new appointment at Dalhousie as professor of English and rhetoric - the art of discourse aiming to improve the capability of writers to inform, persuade or motivate particular audiences in specific situations.

The work for which De Mille is best known today, *A Strange Manuscript Found in a Copper Cylinder, was* serialised posthumously in *Harper's Weekly*, and published in book form by Harper and Brothers of New York City, in 1888. Other famous novels included the 1867 historical novel *Helena's Household: A Tale of Rome in the First Century.* Most of De Mille's books were originally published in serial form, which helped build his public reputation, especially titles such as *The Treasure of the Seas* (1873) and *The Winged Lion* (1877). Aside from his prolific writing, including over twenty-three fictional works and five non-fictional works, De Mille continued to write and teach at Dalhousie until his early death at the age of 47. He died on 28th January, 1880, leaving behind a large oeuvre of celebrated and well-loved works.

THE TORTURE GARDEN
OCTAVE MIRBEAU
(LE JARDIN DES SUPPLICES)
TRANSLATED FROM THE FRENCH
BY ALVAH C. BESSIE

FIRST PUBLISHED 1899

THE MANUSCRIPT

One evening some friends were gathered at the home of one of our most cele-brated writers. Having dined sumptuously, they were discussing murder—apro-pos of what, I no longer remember probably apropos of nothing. Only men were present: moralists, poets, philosophers and doctors—thus everyone could speak freely, according to his whim, his hobby or his idiosyncrasies, without fear of sud-denly seeing that expression of horror and fear which the least startling idea traces upon the horrified face of a notary. I—say notary, much as I might have said lawyer or porter, not disdainfully, of course, but in order to define the average French mind.

With a calmness of spirit as perfect as though he were expressing an opinion upon the merits of the cigar he was smoking, a member of the Academy of Moral and Political Sciences said:

"Really—I honestly believe that murder is the greatest human preoccupation, and that all our acts stem from it... " We awaited the pronouncement of an involved theory, but he remained silent.

"Absolutely!" said a Darwinian scientist, "and, my friend, you are voicing one of those eternal truths such as the legendary Monsieur de La Palisse discovered every day: since murder is the very bedrock of our social institutions, and conse-quently the most imperious necessity of civilized life. If it no longer existed, there would be no governments of any kind, by virtue of the admirable fact that crime in general and murder in particular are not only their excuse, but their only rea-son for being. We should then live in complete anarchy, which is inconceivable. So, instead of seeking to eliminate murder, it is imperative that it be cultivated with intelligence and perseverance. I know no better culture medium than law."

Someone protested. "Here, here!" asked the savant, "aren't we alone, and speak-ing frankly?"

"Please!" said the host, "let us profit thoroughly by the only occasion when we are free to express our personal ideas, for both I, in my books, and you in your turn, may present only lies to the public."

The scientist settled himself once more among the cushions of his armchair, stretched his legs, which were numb from being crossed too long and, his head thrown back, his arms hanging and his stomach soothed by good digestion, puffed smoke-rings at the ceiling:

"Besides," he continued, "murder is largely self-propagating. Actually, it is not the result of this or that passion, nor is it a pathological form of degeneracy. It is a vital instinct which is in us all—which is in all organized beings and dominates them, just as the genetic instinct. And most of the time it is especially true that these two instincts fuse so well, and are so totally interchangeable, that in some way or other they form a single and identical instinct, so that we no longer may tell which of the two urges us to give life, and which to take it—which is murder, and which love. I have been the confidant of an honorable assassin who killed women, not to rob them, but to ravish them. His trick was to manage things *so* that his sexual climax coincided exactly with the death-spasm of the woman: 'At those moments,' he told me, 'I imagined I was a God, creating a world!"

"Ah," cried the celebrated writer, "if you are going to seek your examples among professional assassins—"

"Hold on," the scientist replied; "simply that we are all more or less assassins. I like to believe that, intellectually, we have all experienced analogous sensations to a lesser degree. We restrain the innate need of murder and attenuate physical violence by giving it a legalized outlet: industry, colonial trade, war, the hunt or anti-Semitism, because it is dangerous to abandon oneself to it immoderately and outside the law, and since after all the moral satisfaction we derive from it is not worth exposing ourselves to the ordinary consequences of the act—imprison-ment(testimony before judges (always tiring and scientifically uninteresting), and, finally, the guillotine—"

"You're exaggerating," interrupted the first speaker. "Murder is a dangerous business only for inelegant murderers—witless and impulsive brutes who lack all psychological understanding. An intelligent and rational man may, with ineffable serenity, commit all the murders he desires. He is assured of immunity. The supe-riority of his calculations will always prevail against the routine of police inves-tigation and, let us admit it, against the puerility of the criminal investigations with which presiding magistrates enjoy dabbling. In this business, as in all others, it is the small who pay for the great. Come, my friend, surely you admit that the number of crimes which go unprosecuted—"

"And tolerated—"

"And tolerated—I was about to say that—You will admit that that sum is a thou-sand times greater than the number of discovered and punished crimes ,about which the papers chatter with such strange prolixity, and with so repugnant a lack of understanding. If you will admit that, then concede that the *gendarme* is no hobgoblin to the intellectuals of murder—"

"Undoubtedly—but that's not the question. You are clouding the issue. I said that murder is a normal and not at all exceptional function of nature and all living beings. So it is exorbitant of society, under pretext of governing men, to have abrogated the exclusive right to kill them, to the detriment of the individuals in whom alone this right resides."

"Quite true!" said an amiable and verbose philosopher whose lectures at the Sorbonne draw a select attendance every week. "Our friend is quite right. As far as I am concerned, I do not believe that a human being exists who is not, basical-ly at least, an assassin. Look! when I am in a drawing room, a church, a station; on the *terrasse* of a cafe, at the theatre or wherever crowds pass or loiter, I enjoy considering faces from a strictly homicidal point of view. For you may see by the glance, by the back of the neck, the shape of the skull, the jaw bone and zygoma of the cheeks, or by some part of their persons that they bear the stigmata of that psychological calamity known as murder. It is scarcely an aberration of my mind, but I can go nowhere without seeing it flickering beneath eyelids, or without feeling its mysterious contact in the touch of every hand held out to me.

Last Sunday I went to a town on the festival day of its patron saint. In the public square, which was decorated with foliage, floral arches, and poles draped with flags, was grouped every kind of amusement common to that sort of public celebration—And beneath the paternal eye of the authorities, a swarm of good people were enjoying themselves. The wooden horses, the roller-coaster and the swings drew a very meager crowd. The organs wheezed their gayest tunes and most bewitching overtures in vain. Other pleasures absorbed this festive throng. Some shot with rifles, pistols, or the good old cross-bow at targets painted like human faces; others hurled balls, knocking over marionettes ranged pathetically on wooden bars. Still others, mallet in hand, pounded upon a spring which animated a French sailor who patriotically transfixed with his bayonet a poor Hova or a mocking Dahomean. Everywhere, under tents or in the little lighted booths, I saw counterfeits of death, parodies of massacre, portrayals of hecatombs. And how happy these good people were!"

Everyone realized the philosopher was launched upon his subject, so we settled ourselves as best we could, to withstand the torrent of his theories and anecdotes. He continued:

"I notice that these gentle pastimes have for some years been undergoing a considerable development. The joy of killing has become greater and, besides, has become popularized in proportion to the spread of social refinement—for make no mistake, customs do change! Formerly, when we were still uncultivated, the Sabbath shooting-galleries were a monotonously sorry sight to see. They only shot at pipes, and eggshells dancing upon jets of water. In the more sumptuous establishments, they actually had birds, but they were made of plaster. I ask you what fun was there in that? Today, progress has made it legal for every good man to procure himself the delicate and edifying emotion of assassination, for a couple of *sous*. Into the bargain, you may still win colored plates and rabbits; but, instead of pipes, eggshells, and plaster birds, which smash stupidly without suggesting anything bloody to us, the showman's imagination has substituted figures of men, women and children, carefully jointed and costumed as they should be. Then they have made these figures gesticulate and walk. By means of an ingenious mechanism, they walk happily along, or flee terrified. You see them appear alone or in groups, in decorative settings, scaling walls, entering dungeons, tumbling out of windows, popping up out of trapdoors... They function just like real beings and move their arms, legs and heads. Some appear to be weeping, some seem to be paupers, some invalids, and there are some dressed in gold like legendary princesses. Really, you can believe that they possess intelligence, a will, a soul—that they are alive! Some even assume pathetic attitudes. You can almost hear them cry: 'Mercy! Don't kill me!' It is an exquisite sensation to imagine you are going to kill things that move, suffer, and implore! Something like a taste of warm blood comes to your mouth when you aim the rifle or the pistol at them. What a thrill when the shot decapitates these make-believe men! What a clamor when the arrow splits their cardboard breasts and lays the little inanimate bodies low, in corpse-like postures! Everybody gets excited, intent, and eggs the others on. You hear nothing but expressions of destruction and death: 'Kill him!' 'Aim at his eye, aim at his heart!' 'He got his!' No matter how indifferent these good people are to the targets and the pipes, they become elated when the mark represents a human being. The clumsy ones grow angry, not with their own awkwardness, but with the marionette they have missed. They call it a coward and overwhelm it with vile insults when it disappears intact behind the door of a dungeon. They challenge it: 'Come on out, you bum!' They begin to fire at it again, until they have killed it. Consider these good people; at that moment they are really assassins, beings moved solely by the desire to kill. The homicidal monster which up to then had slumbered in them, awakens with the illusion that they are going to destroy something living.

"For, the little fellow of cardboard, sawdust, or wood which moves back and forth amid the scenery is no longer a toy to them, or a bit of lifeless material. Watching it pass back and forth, they unconsciously endow it with warm blood, sensitive nerves, thought—all those things it is so bitterly sweet to annihilate and so fiercely delicious to see oozing from the wounds you have inflicted. They even go so far as to ascribe political and religious convictions to it, contrary to their own; accusing it of being a Jew, an Englishman, or a German, in order to add a particular hate to this general hatred of life, and thus augment the instinctive pleasure of killing by a personal vengeance, intimately relished."

Here the host interrupted out of politeness to his guests, and with the charitable desire of permitting our philosopher and us a breathing space. He objected, quietly:

"You're only talking of brutes—peasants who, I concede, are always inclined toward murder. But it is not possible for you to apply the same observations to cultivated minds, disciplined natures, or cultured individuals every day of whose lives witnesses victories over native instinct and the savage vestiges of atavism."

To which our philosopher eagerly replied:

"Allow me—what are the habits, my friend, and the preferred pleasures of those whom you call 'cultivated minds and disciplined natures'? Fencing, dueling, violent sports, the abominable pigeon-shoot, bull fighting, the various manifestations of patriotism, hunting—everything which is in reality only a reversion to the period of old-time barbarity, when man—if we may say so was, as far as moral culture is concerned, on the same plane with the wild beasts he pursued. After all, we need not complain that the hunt has survived all the slightly altered trappings of earlier customs. It is a powerful counter-irritant, through whose agency 'cultivated minds and disciplined natures' are enabled, without too much harm to us, to drain off what destructive energy and bloody passion still remains in them. Without it, instead of coursing deer, finishing off the boar and slaughtering innocent game-birds in the meadows, you may be sure that the 'cultivated minds would turn their packs on our trail. We would be the ones whom the 'disciplined natures' would joyfully mow down with rifle-fire, which they do not fail to do when they obtain the power, through some means or another, and with more determination and—let us frankly admit it—less hypocrisy than the brute peasant. Ah, let us never look forward to the disappearance of game from our fields and forests! It is our safeguard and, after a fashion, our ransom. The day it finally disappears, it will not be long before we take its place, for the exquisite enjoyment of the 'cultivated minds'. The Dreyfus affair affords us an excellent example, and never, I believe, was the passion for murder and the joy of the manhunt so thoroughly and cynically displayed. The pursuit of Monsieur Grimaux through the streets of Nantes remains the most characteristic of the startling incidents and monstrous events to which it gave opportunity daily during the past year. And it accrues to the honor of the 'cultivated minds and disciplined natures', who saw to it that this great savant, to whom we are indebted for the most brilliant researches in chemistry, was overwhelmed with indignities and threats of death. In this connection, we must always remember that the mayor of Clisson, 'a cultivated mind', in a letter which was made public, refused to allow Monsieur Grimaux to enter his town, and regretted that modern laws did not permit him to hang him high and dry—a thing which befell savants in the lovely days of the ancient monarchies. And for that, this excellent mayor was strongly commended by all whom France numbers among those exquisite 'worldly personalities' who, according to our host, win such brilliant victories every day over original instinct and the savage vestiges of atavism. Notice also that it is from among the cultivated minds and disciplined natures that officers are almost exclusively recruited. Men—that is to say—who, neither more nor less wicked nor stupid than others, freely choose a calling—a highly honored calling, moreover—in which every intellectual effort is bent toward committing the most diversified violations upon the human being; and in developing and compiling the most complete, far reaching and certain means of pillage, destruction and death. Aren't there warships to which we have given the perfectly logical and understandable names of *Devastation... Fury... Terror*?

"As for me? Listen to this! I'm positive that I believe I am a normal man, with affections, high sentiments, superior culture and the refinements of civilization and sociability. Well, how often have I heard the imperious voice of murder snarling in me! How often have I felt the desire rising in a surge of blood from the depths of my being to my brain—that bitter, violent and almost invincible desire to kill. Do not believe that this desire arose in a passionate crisis, accompanied a sudden, unreflective rage, or was combined with a keen lust for money. Not at all!

This desire is born suddenly—powerful and unjustified in me—for no reason and apropos of nothing... In the street, for example, behind the back of an unknown pedestrian. Yes, there are some backs on the street which cry for the knife. Why?" After this unexpected revelation, the philosopher was silent for a moment, and looked at us all in alarm; then he continued:

"No—you see, the moralists have split hairs in vain. The need to kill is born in man with the need to eat, and merges with it... This instinctive need, which is the mainspring of all living organisms, is developed by education instead of being restrained, and is sanctified by religion instead of being denounced. Everything conspires to make it the pivot upon which our admirable society revolves. As soon as man awakens to consciousness, we instill the spirit of murder in his mind. Murder, expanded to the status of a duty, and popularized to the point of heroism, accompanies him through all the stages of his existence. He is made to adore uncouth gods, mad, furious gods who are only gratified by cataclysms and, ferocious maniacs that they are, gorge themselves with human lives and mow down nations like fields of wheat. He is made to respect only heroes, those disgusting brutes saddled with crime and red with human blood. The virtues by which he rises above others, and which win him glory, fortune and love, are based entirely upon murder. In war, he discovers the supreme synthesis of the eternal and everlasting folly of murder—regulated, regimented and obligatory—a national function. Wherever he goes, whatever he does, he will always see that word: murder—immortally inscribed upon the pediment of that vast slaughter-house—humanity.

"Then why do you expect this man, in whom the scorn of human life is inculcated from infancy, and whom we consecrate to legalized slaughter—why do you expect him to recoil from murder when he finds in it interest or distraction? In the name of what law could society condemn assassins who, in reality, have only conformed to the homicidal laws which it dictates, and followed the bloody example which it sets them? 'Why is it?' assassins might readily say, 'that you force us to overpower groups of men whom we do not hate, whom we do not even know—then, the more we overwhelm them, the more you overwhelm us with rewards and honors? Then again, trusting in your logic, we destroy people because they hamper us or we detest them, or because we covet their money, their wives, their positions, or simply because we enjoy destroying them: all of which are concise, plausible and human reasons—and along comes the *gendarme*, the judge and the hangman! 'Here is a revolting injustice which is perfectly senseless!' What could society reply to that, if it had the slightest regard for logic?"

A young man who had been silent until then said:

"Is this really the explanation of that strange murderous mania by which you maintain we are all originally or willfully tainted? I do not think so and I do not wish to. I prefer to believe that everything about us is mysterious. Furthermore, this satisfies the indolence of my mind, which has a horror of solving social, and human problems which, besides, are never solved. And it strengthens the reasons—the purely poetic reasons by which I am tempted to explain, or rather not to explain, everything which I do not understand. You have just made quite a terrible disclosure, Doctor, and described impressions which, if they were to assume active form, might lead you far a field, and me also; for I have often experienced these impressions, and quite recently, under the following exceptionally banal circumstances. But first permit me to add that I ascribe these abnormal states of mind to the environment in which I was brought up, and the daily influences which affected me, unawares.

"You know my father, Doctor Trepan. You know that there is no more sociable or charming man than he. Nor is there one of whom the profession has made a more deliberate assassin. I have often witnessed those marvelous operations which made him famous the world over. There is something truly phenomenal in his disregard for life. Once he had just performed a difficult laparotomy and, examining his patient, who was still under the influence of the chloroform, he suddenly said: "This woman may have an affected pylorus... suppose I also go into that stomach. I have time. Which he did. There was nothing wrong. Then my father started to sew up the needless wound he had made, saying: 'Now, at least, I'm certain.' He was so certain that the patient died the very same night. Another time, in Italy, where he had been summoned for an operation, we were visiting a museum. I was enraptured. 'Ah, poet! poet!' exclaimed my father, who was not interested for a moment in the masterpieces which carried me away with enthusiasm; 'Art! art! Beauty! Do you know what it is? Well, my boy, it is a woman's abdomen, open and all bloody, with the hemostats in place!' But I won't philosophize any more, I'll narrate... From the tale I promised you, you will deduce all the anthropological conclusions of which it admits, if it really admits of any..."

This young man had So authoritative a manner and so bitter a tone, that it made us shiver slightly.

"I was returning from Lyon," he continued, "and I was alone in a first-class compartment. I've forgotten what station it was, but a traveler got on. I admit that the irritation of being disturbed when alone can bring about very violent states of mind, and arouse you to peevish behavior. But I experienced nothing of the sort. I was so bored with being alone that the chance arrival of this companion was rather a pleasure to me from the very start. He settled himself across from me, after carefully depositing his few bags in the rack. He was a bulky man, of common appearance, whose greasy ugliness shortly became obnoxious to me. After a few moments, I felt something like an insuperable disgust in looking at him. He was stretched opt heavily on the cushions, his thighs apart, and at every jolt of the train his enormous belly trembled and heaved like a disgusting mass of jelly. As he seemed hot, he took off his collar and sloppily mopped his forehead—a low, wrinkled and bumpy forehead, raggedly framed by a few short, sticky hairs. His face was merely a lumpy mass of fat; his triple chin a slack flap of soft flesh, spread on his chest. To avoid this unpleasant sight I pretended to look at the countryside, and forcibly tore myself away from the presence of this irksome companion. An hour passed. And when curiosity, stronger than my will, had drawn my eyes back to him, I saw that he had fallen into a deep and unprepossessing sleep. He slept, sunk into himself, his head drooping and rolling upon his shoulders, and his huge, bloated hands lay open upon the slopes of his thighs. I noticed that his round eyes bulged beneath creased eyelids, and that a bit of bluish pupil showed through a slit, like an ecchymosis on a scrap of limp veal. What insane idea suddenly flashed through my mind? Truly, I don't know. For though I had been frequently tempted by murder, it lay in me in an embryonic state of desire, and had never as yet assumed the precise form of a gesture or an act. Is it possible that the ignominious ugliness of this man alone was able to crystallize that gesture and that act? No, there is a more profound cause, of which I am ignorant. I arose quietly and approached the sleeper, my hands spread, contracted and violent, as though to strangle him."

With these words, being a story-teller who knew how to get his effects, he paused. Then, evidently satisfied with himself, he continued:

"Despite my rather puny appearance, I am gifted with unusual strength, exceptional muscular agility, and extraordinary power of grip, and at that moment a strange heat unleashed the dynamic force of my bodily faculties. My hands alone moved towards this man's neck—by themselves, I assure you—burning and terrible. I felt in me a lightness, an elasticity, an influx of nervous tides, something like the powerful intoxication of sexual desire. Yes, I can't explain what I felt better than to compare it with that. The minute my hands were about to close upon this greasy neck, the man woke up. He awoke with terror in his eyes, and he stuttered: 'What? what? what?' And that was all! I saw that he wanted to say more, but he couldn't! His round eye flickered like a little light sputtering in the wind. Then it remained fixed and motionless upon me, in horror. Without saying a word, without even seeking an excuse or a reason, by which the man would have been reassured, I sat down again across from him and nonchalantly, with an ease of manner which still astonishes me, I unfolded a newspaper which, however, I did not read. Fear grew in the man's eyes with every moment; little by little he recoiled, and I saw his face grow spotted with red, then purple, then it stiffened. All the way to Paris, the man's stare retained its frightful fixity. When the train stopped, the man did not get off... " The narrator lit a cigarette in the flame of a candle, and from a cloud of smoke his phlegmatic voice was saying:

"Oh, I know well enough. I had killed him! He was dead of cerebral congestion."

This story made us very uneasy, and we looked at each other stupefied. Was the strange young man sincere? Had he tried to mystify us? We awaited an explanation, a commentary or an evasion, but he was silent. Grave and serious, he had resumed smoking, and now he seemed to be thinking of something else. From then on the conversation continued chaotic and lifeless, skimming a thousand frivolous subjects in a languid manner.

Then a man with a ravaged face, a bowed back and mournful eyes, whose hair and beard were prematurely grey, arose with difficulty and in a trembling voice, said:

"Up to now you nave talked of everything but women, which is really inconceivable in a situation in which they are of primary importance."

"Fine! Let's talk about them," agreed the illustrious writer, who now found himself in his favorite environment; for in the literary world he passed for that curious fool called a feminist writer. "It's high time that all these bloody nightmares were infused with a little jollity. Let us talk of woman, my friends, since it is by her and through her that we forget our savage instincts—that we learn to love, and are raised to the supreme conception of pity and the idea!"

The man with the ravaged face emitted a rasping, ironical laugh.

"Woman, teacher of compassion!" he exclaimed; "Yes, I know the anthem. It is utilized a good deal in a certain type of literature, and in courses in drawing-room philosophy. Why, her entire history, and not only her history, but her role in nature and life contradicts this purely romantic concept. Why do women rush to bloody spectacles with the same frenzy that they fly to the pursuit of passion? Why is it that you see them in the streets, at the theatre, in the court of assizes or beside the guillotine, craning their necks and eagerly straining their eyes to sights of torture, in order to experience, to the swooning-point, the frightful thrill of death? Why does the very name of a great assassin make them tremble to the very depths of their flesh with a sort of delicious horror? All of them, or nearly all, dreamed about Pranzini! Why?"

"Nonsense!" exclaimed the illustrious writer. "Prostitutes—"

"No," said the man with the ravaged face, "noblewomen—and bourgeoisies—it's the same thing. Among women there are no moral categories—only social categories. They are women. Among the common people and in the upper and lower middle-class, and right on up to the most elevated social strata, women pounce upon those hideous morgues and abject museums of crime that make up the fiction columns of the *Petit Journal*. Why? Because great assassins have always been formidable lovers. Their genetic powers equal their criminal powers. They love in the same way they kill! Murder is born of love, and love attains its greatest intensity in murder. There is the same physiological exaltation, there are the same gestures of strangling and biting—and often the same words occur during identical spasms." He spoke with difficulty, with an air of suffering and as he spoke his eyes became more mournful and the wrinkles in his face were more accentuated.

Woman, dispenser of ideality and compassion!" he went on: "Why, the most atrocious crimes are nearly always the work of woman. It is she who conceives them, organizes them, prepares them and directs them. If she does not execute them with her own hands, which are often too weak, you find her moral presence, her ideas, and her sex expressed in their ferocity and implacability. 'Look for the woman!' said the wise criminologist."

"You slander her!" protested the author, who could not conceal a gesture of indignation. "What you offer us as generalizations are the very rare exceptions. Degeneracy... neurosis... neurasthenia... My God! Woman is no more impervious to psychical disease than man—although with her these disturbances assume a charming and touching form, which makes us better understand the delicacy of her exquisite tenderness. No sir, you have fallen into a deplorable error. To the contrary, what we must admire in woman is her great common sense and her great love of life which, as I said before, finds its final expression in compassion."

"Literature, sir, literature! "And the worst possible kind!"

"Pessimism, sir! Blasphemy! Stupidity!"

"I think both of you are mistaken," interrupted a physician; "women are far more specialized and complete than you think. Incomparable virtuosi and great artists in grief that they are, they prefer the sight of suffering to that of death, and tears to blood. And it's a wonderfully ambiguous business in which each finds what he is looking for; since everyone draws quite different conclusions. We exalt woman's compassion or curse her cruelty for equally irrefutable reasons, according to whether we are momentarily disposed to owe her gratitude or hatred. So what good are all these fruitless discussions; for in the eternal battle of the sexes, we are always conquered—and we can do nothing about it—and none of us as yet, be he misogynist or feminist, has found a more perfect instrument of pleasure, or any other means of reproduction, than woman."

But the man with the ravaged face made violent gestures of denial:

"Listen to me," he said. "The hazards of existence and what a life *I've* had—have placed me in the presence of—not *a* woman—but *woman*. I have seen her, stripped of the artifices and hypocrisies with which civilization veils her real soul. I have seen her abandoned to her single whim, or, if you prefer, to her sole driving instincts, in an environment where nothing, it is true, can restrain them and, on the contrary, everything conspires to excite them. Neither laws, morals, religious prejudices nor social conventions hid her from me—nothing. It was her true self I saw, in her original ,nudity, among gardens and tortures—blood and flowers! When she appeared to me I had fallen to the lowest point of human abjection—at least, I thought so. Then, before her amorous eyes and her compassionate mouth I cried out with hope, and I believed—yes, I believed that through her I would be saved. Well, it was something fearful! Woman revealed crimes to me that I had not known! shadows into which I had not yet descended. Look at my dead eyes, my inarticulate lips, my hands which tremble—only from what I have seen! But I can no more curse her than I can curse the fire which devours towns and forests, the waters which sink ships, or the tiger which carries his bloody prey in his jaws into the depths of the jungle. Woman possesses the cosmic force of an element, an invincible force of destruction, like nature's. She is, in herself alone,

all nature! Being the matrix of life, she is by that very fact the matrix of death—
since it is from death that life is perpetually reborn, and since to annihilate death
would be to kill life at its only fertile source."

"What does that prove?" said the doctor, shrugging his shoulders.

He answered simply:

"It proves nothing. Must things be proved in order to be painful or pleasant?
They need only be felt..."

Then, timidly and—oh, the power of human vanity!—with visible self-satisfac-
tion, the man with the ravaged face took out of his pocket a roll of paper, which
he carefully unfolded:

"I have written," he said, "the story of this period of my life. I have hesitated to
publish it for a long time, and I still hesitate. I would like to read it to you—you
who are men and have no fear of plumbing the blackest of human mysteries. May
you be able to withstand its bloody horror! It is called: TORTURE GARDEN..."

Our host called for fresh cigars and fresh drinks.

THE MISSION
PART 1

Before relating one of the most frightful episodes of my travels in the Far East, perhaps it will be interesting if I briefly explain under what conditions I was led to undertake them. It is contemporary history.

To those who will be tempted to wonder at the anonymity which I have insisted on jealously maintaining in what concerns me in the course of this authentic and distressing story, I will say: "My name matters little; it is the name of a man who has caused great suffering to others as well as to himself—even more to himself than to others—and who, after many shocks suffered in a descent to the very dregs of human desire, is trying to reconstruct a soul for himself in solitude and obscurity. Peace to the ashes of his sin."

Twelve years ago, no longer knowing what to do, and condemned by a series of misfortunes to the cruel expedient of hanging myself or throwing myself into the Seine, I appeared before that court of last resort, the board of legislative elections, in a county in which, more over, I knew no one and had never set foot.

It is true that my candidacy was officially supported by the cabinet which, no longer knowing what to do with me, found an ingenious and polite means of relieving itself once and for all of my daily harassing importunities.

On this occasion I held a solemn and intimate interview with the Minister, who was my friend and old school-chum.

"You see how nice we are to you!" this powerful, this generous friend said to me; "Scarcely have we snatched you from the jaws of justice—and we had a hard time doing it—than we're making you a deputy."

"I'm not nominated yet," I said peevishly.

"True! but you have every chance. Intelligent, of attractive appearance, debonair, and a good fellow when you care to be, you possess the sovereign gift of pleasing. Ladies' men, my boy, are always men of the people. I'll vouch for you. It's a question of properly understanding the situation. The rest is very simple." And he admonished me:

"Above all, rid politics! Don't commit yourself. Don't fly off the handle! In the district I have chosen for you there is one question that supersedes all others: the beet. The rest doesn't count, and is the prefect's business. You are a purely agricultural candidate—more than that, exclusively a beet-candidate. Don't forget it for a moment. Whatever may happen in die course of the campaign, stand resolutely upon this excellent platform. Do you know anything about beets?" "Good Lord no!" I said, "except, like everybody else, I know you get sugar from them—and alcohol."

"Bravo! That's enough," applauded the Minister, with friendly and reassuring emphasis. "proceed upon that data. Promise fabulous crops—extraordinary chemical fertilizers—free. Promise railroads, canals, routes for the transportation of this interesting and patriotic vegetable. Announce reductions in taxes, bonuses for the farmers, atrocious duties on competitive products—anything you like! You have carte blanche in this affair, and I'll help you. But don't get involved in personal or generalized polemics which might endanger you and, after your election, imperil the prestige of the Republic. For, between you and me, old man—I don't reproach you with any thing—I merely state facts—you have a rather awkward past."

I was in no mood to laugh. Vexed by this after-thought, which seemed to me unnecessary and unkind, I replied sharply, looking my friend squarely in the face; and he could read the cold, sharp threats that lay in my eyes:

You might more truthfully have said, 'We have a past.' It seems to me, my friend, that mine has nothing on yours."

"Oh, as for me!" said the Minister, with an air of superior detachment and smug nonchalance, "it's not the same thing... I, old man—France covers my tracks!" Then, returning to my election, he added:

"Now I'll continue. Beets—more beets—and still more beets! Such is your program. And see that you don't deviate from it." Then he discreetly gave me some money and wished me good luck.

I faithfully followed this program which my powerful friend had laid out for me, and I was wrong. I was not elected. I attribute the overwhelming majority which my adversary received, aside from certain dishonest manipulations, to the fact that this wretch was even more ignorant than I, and a more notorious blackguard. Let us notice, in passing, that at the present time a well-displayed swinishness supersedes all valid qualifications, and the more infamous a man is, the more we are inclined to endow him with intellectual force and moral courage.

My adversary, who is today one of the indisputable glories of politics, had pilfered on many occasions. And his superiority may be attributed to the fact that instead of concealing his speculations, he boasted of them with the most revolting cynicism.

"I've stolen! I've stolen!" he shouted down village streets, in public squares, along the countryside and across the fields.

"I've stolen! I've stolen!" he proclaimed in his professions of faith, his billposters and confidential circulars. And in cabarets his agents, perched upon casks, spattered with wine and bloated with alcohol, reiterated and bellowed those magic words:

"He's stolen! He's stolen!"

The working classes in the cities, dazzled no less than the sturdy countrymen, acclaimed this bold man with a frenzy which swelled in direct proportion to die frenzy of his confessions.

How could I contend with such a rival, who possessed such qualifications—I, who still had on my conscience (and modestly concealed them), merely the paltry peccadilloes of youth: petty thefts, extortion of money from mistresses, cheating at games, blackmail, anonymous letters, informing and forgery? Oh, the candor of innocent youth!

One evening at a mass-meeting I even barely escaped being thrashed by some electors who were furious because, in view of my, opponent's scandalous statements, I had demanded—in addition to better beets—the right to be virtuous, moral and honest, and proclaimed the necessity of cleansing the Republic of the particular filth which dishonored it. They rushed upon me, grasped me by the throat, and my body was lifted and tossed from hand to hand, like a bundle. Luckily I escaped from the consequences of my excess of eloquence with only a swollen cheek, three bruised ribs and six broken teeth.

That is all I carried away from that disastrous adventure into which the protection of the Minister who claimed to be my friend had so unluckily led me. I was incensed.

I had all the more right to be incensed since, suddenly, in the thick of the battle, the government had abandoned me, leaving me without support, and with only my beet as an amulet by which to make myself understood and to parley with my adversary.

The prefect, at first quite humble, did not hesitate to become very insolent; then he refused me the data upon which my campaign rested, and finally he almost slammed his door in my face. The Minister himself no longer answered my letters, refused to grant me anything I asked him, and the partisan newspapers launched underhand attacks upon me and made derogatory allusions couched in polished and flowery prose, They never went so far as to attack me officially, but it was plain to everyone that I was being dismissed. Ah, I truly believe that no man has ever been so embittered as I!

I returned to Paris firmly resolved to raise an issue at the risk of losing everything, and demanded an explanation of the Minister, whom my belligerent attitude immediately reduced to compliance and amiability.

"Old man," he said, "I regret what has happened to you. On my word of honor! You can see for yourself I'm miserable about it. But what could I do? I am not the only man in the cabinet, and—"

"You're the only one I know!" I interrupted violently, upsetting piles of papers which lay near me on his desk. "The others don't concern me. The others are none of my business. You're the only one. You've betrayed me—it's vile!"

"But damn it, listen a minute, will you!" begged the Minister, "and don't get angry like that before you know—"

"I only know one thing, and that's enough for me. You've made a fool of me. Well then—no, no, it won't pass off as easily as you think. It's my turn now." I walked up and down the office, uttering threats and kicking the chairs.

"So! so! you've made a fool of me! Now we're going to have some fun! Then the country will know at last what a Minister is. At the risk of poisoning it, I'll show it—I'll expose the soul of a Minister to it. Idiot! So you didn't realize that you, your career, your secrets, and your portfolio, are at my mercy! So my past troubles you? It shocks your modesty, and Marianne's? Just wait! Tomorrow—yes, tomorrow, everything will be known—"

I was choking with rage. The Minister tried to calm me, grasped me by the arm and drew me gently, into the armchair I had just bounded out of in fury.

"Calm down!" he said to me, and his voice too on a pleading tone. "Listen to me, please! Come, sit down! Stubborn ass! You won't listen to anything! Here, this is what happened..."

He uttered swift, short sentences, choppy and trembling:

We reckoned without your opponent. In the campaign he revealed himself a powerful man—a real statesman! You know how restricted the eligible ministerial personnel is. Although the same candidates are always coming up, from time to time we have to show a new face to the Chamber and the country. Well, there is none. Do you know any? Well, we thought your opponent might be one of those faces. He has all the qualities suitable to a provisory Minister—an emergency Minister. Finally, since he was for sale and deliverable right then and there—you understand? It's hard on you, I admit... But the country's welfare, first of all—"

"Don't talk nonsense. We're not in the Chamber now, It's not a question of the country's interests, which You don't give a damn about, and neither do I. It's a question of me. Well, thanks to you, I'm on the street. Yesterday the cashier of my gambling-joint insolently refused me a hundred sous. My creditors, banking on my success and furious at my defeat, are hounding me like a hare. I'll be sold out! Today, I haven't even the price of a dinner. And you simply imagine that things can go on like this? Well, have you become senseless—as senseless as a member of the majority?"

The Minister smiled. He tapped me familiarly on the knee and said:

"I'm entirely willing—but you won't let me speak—I'm entirely willing to grant you a compensation—"

"A reparation!"

"A reparation, agreed!"

"Complete?"

"Complete! Come back in a few days... Doubtless I'll be in a position to offer it to you then. In the meantime here's a hundred louis. It's all I have left of the confidential funds."

Sweetly, with merry cordiality, he added:

"A half-a-dozen more guys like you, and there'll be no budget!"

This generosity, which had exceeded my expectations, possessed the power instantly to calm my nerves. Still grumbling incessantly, for I did not wish to appear disarmed or satisfied, I pocketed the two bills my friend smilingly held out to me, and I retired with dignity.

I spent the following three days in the basest debauchery.

PART 2

Permit me to go back once more into the past. Perhaps it is not immaterial that

I tell you who I am and where I come from. It will explain the irony of my fate so much better.

I was born in the country, of a lower middle-class family—that honest, thrifty and virtuous middle-class which, they inform us in official bulletins, is the real France. Oh well, I am none the prouder for that.

My father was a grain merchant. He was a very crude, uncultured man, and a very astute business man. He had the reputation of being very clever, and this great cleverness consisted of 'roping people in' as he used to say. To cheat about the quality and weight of merchandise; to charge two francs for what cost him two sous and whenever possible, without raising too much of a scandal, to get those two francs twice—such were his principles. For instance, he never delivered oats that he had not first soaked with water. In that way, the swollen grains yielded double measure to the liter or kilogram, especially when a little gravel had been added—a practice which my father always indulged in conscientiously. He also knew how discreetly to distribute in the bags blighted and other noxious seeds thrown off in threshing—and no one could adulterate fresh flour with fermented better than he. For in business, nothing must be wasted, and everything makes weight. My mother, who was even more greedy for dishonest profits, assisted him by her predatory ingenuity and sat stiff and distrustful, watching over the till as one mounts guard before an enemy.

A strict Republican and a fiery patriot—he furnished supplies to the army—an intolerant moralist and a good man after all, in the popular sense of the word, my father had no pity and accepted no excuse for the dishonesty of others; especially when it was to his disadvantage. In such cases he could never cease talking about the necessity for honor and virtue. One of his great ideas was that in a well-organized democracy they should be made compulsory—like education, taxes and voting. One day he discovered that a teamster who had been in his service for fifteen years, was robbing him. He immediately had him arrested. At the trial the teamster defended himself as best he could:

"But the boss never hesitated to 'rope people in'. Whenever he had played a good trick on a customer, he boasted about it as though he had done a good deed. 'The only thing is to take in the cash,' he used to say, 'no matter where or how you get it. To sell a dead cat for a live horse—that's the secret of business.' Well, I've done just what the boss does with his customers. I've roped him in."

These cynical remarks made a bad impression on the judges. They sentenced the teamster to two years in prison, not only for having pilfered a few kilograms of grain, but chiefly because he had slandered one of the oldest business houses in district... a house founded in 1794, whose long-standing, steadfast, and legendary respectability had been the ornament of the town from generation to generation.

I remember that on the evening of this celebrated decision my father had gathered some friends at table: merchants like himself and, like him, rooted in this inaugural principle that to 'rope people in' was the very soul of trade. You can imagine how indignant they were about the defiant attitude of the teamster. They talked of nothing else until midnight; and out of the confusion, epigrams, discussions and little glasses of brandy, I distilled this precept: which was, so to speak, the moral of the episode and at the same time the synthesis of my education:

To take something from a person and keep it for one self: that is robbery. To take something from one person and then turn it over to another in exchange for as much money as you can get: that is business. Robbery is so much more stupid, since it is satisfied with a single, frequently dangerous profit; whereas in business it Can be doubled without danger.

It was in this moral atmosphere that in some way or other I grew up and developed entirely alone, with no other text than the daily example of my parents. Among the shop keeping classes children are generally left to their own devices, for no one has time to bother with their education. They educate themselves as best they can, at the mercy of their own dispositions and the pernicious influences of that environment, which is generally degrading and confined. Spontaneously, and without the need of any outward pressure, I contributed my own portion of emulation or invention to the family swindles. From the age of ten I had no other concept of life than theft, and I was convinced—oh, quite ingenuously I assure you—that to 'rope people in' constituted the foundation of all social intercourse.

College determined the bizarre and tortuous direction I was to give to my own life, for it was there I met the man who was later to become my friend—the celebrated Minister, Eugene Mortain.

The son of a wine-merchant, groomed for politics (just as I was for business) by his father, who was the chief electoral representative of the district, vice-president of the Gambettist committees and founder of various leagues, opposition groups and professional syndicates, Eugene bore within him from infancy the soul of 'a born statesman'.

Although the recipient of a free scholarship, he immediately overawed us with his obvious superiority in effrontery and rudeness, and also by a solemn and vacuous manner of speaking which did violence to our enthusiasms. Besides, he inherited from his father the profitable and efficacious mania for organization. In a few weeks he had made short work of transforming, the college campus into a meeting place for all sorts of societies and clubs, committees and sub-committees, of which he simultaneously elected himself president, secretary and treasurer. There was the football association, the top association, the leap-frog society, and the walking dub; there was the horizontal-bar committee, the trapeze league, the one-legged race syndicate, etc. Every member of these various associations was obliged to contribute to the general fund—that is to say, our comrade's pockets—monthly dues of five sous which, among other advantages, entitled him to a subscription to the quarterly journal which Eugene Mortain edited as propaganda for the ideas, and the defense of the interests, of the numerous 'autonomous and solitary groups,' as he proclaimed.

Evil instincts and appetites which were common to us both immediately bound us together and made of our close partnership a greedy and incessant exploitation of our comrades, who were proud to be syndicated. I soon discovered I was the lesser power in this duplicity, but the realization of this fact made me cling only the aster to the career of this ambitious companion. As compensation for lack of an equal division. I was always assured of being able to pick up a few crumbs... they sufficed me then. Alas! I have never had more than the crumbs of the cakes my friend devoured.

I rediscovered Eugene later, during a difficult and distressing episode of my life. By dint of 'roping people in' my father had ended by being roped in himself, and not in the figurative sense which he applied to his customers. An unfortunate stock of provisions which, it appeared, poisoned an entire barracks, was the occasion for this deplorable incident, which crowned the total ruin of our house founded in 1794. My father might perhaps have survived his dishonor, for he was aware of the infinite indulgence of his epoch; but he could not survive his ruin. An attack of apoplexy carried him off one beautiful evening. He died, leaving my mother and me penniless.

No longer able to count on him, I was definitely obliged to get myself out of the mess alone and, tearing myself away from the maternal lamentations, I fled to Paris where Eugene Mortain welcomed me with open arms.

That worthy was rising little by little. Thanks to parliamentary protection, cleverly exploited, to the agility of his nature and his absolute lack of scruples, he was beginning to be well spoken of in the press, and in political and financial circles. He immediately employed me to do his dirty work, nor was it long before, living as I did in his shadow, I absorbed some of his notoriety, by which I did not know how to profit as I should have. But I was most lacking in the ability to persevere in wrongdoing. Not that I experienced belated qualms of conscience, remorse or fleeting desires for honesty: there is a diabolical streak in me, a relentless and inexplicable perversity which suddenly forces me, without apparent reason, to drop the best conducted of affairs and loosen my hold on the most greedily gripped throats. With practical qualities of the very first order, an acute flair for life, the audacity even to conceive the impossible and an exceptional alacrity in materializing it, I still have not the necessary tenacity of a man of action. Perhaps beneath the scoundrel that I am, there lies a misled poet? Perhaps a mystifier who enjoys mystifying himself?

However, in foreknowledge of the future, and feeling that the day would inevitably come when my friend Eugene would want to get rid of a man who symbolized to him an embarrassing past, I had the cunning to compromise him by circulating derogatory stories, and the foresight to keep in my possession incontrovertible proofs. For fear of a downfall, Eugene was forced perpetually to drag me about after him like a ball and chain.

While awaiting the supreme honors towards which the muddy stream of politics was bearing him, here, among other honorable matters, were the nature of his intrigues and the subjects of his preoccupation:

Officially, Eugene had a mistress. She was then known as the Countess Borska. Not very young, but still pretty and desirable, now a Pole, now a Russian and frequently an Austrian, she naturally passed for a German spy. Therefore her salon was a hangout for most of our illustrious statesmen. Many political affairs were bandied about there, and amid considerable coquetry, many notable and dubious transactions found their inception. Among the most frequent guests of this salon, a certain Levantine financier, Baron K—, was conspicuous. He was a quiet man, with a wan grey face and dull eyes, who had revolutionized the Stock Exchange by his formidable manipulations. It was known, or at least it was said, that behind this silent and impenetrable mask one of the most powerful Empires of Europe was in operation. It was doubtless a purely romantic concept, for in these corrupt places one never knows which to admire more—their corruption or their insipidity. Nevertheless, Countess Borska and my friend entertained lively hopes of being taken into the confidence of the mysterious baron, and continued to hope all the more energetically as the latter opposed their discreet but definite advances, with an even more discreet and definite reserve. I even believe that he pushed his reserve so far as to give them malicious advice, which resulted in a disastrous transaction for our friends. Then they conceived of letting loose upon the recalcitrant banker a very pretty young woman, who was an intimate friend of their household, and to let me loose at the same time upon the very pretty young woman who, worked upon by them, was quite willing to accept us favorably—the banker for business, and me for pleasure. Their calculation was simple and I grasped it at the very start: introduce me into the place and there I, through the woman, and they through me, would become roasters of the secrets which the baron let slip in moments of tender forgetfulness! This is what might be called high-pressure politics!

Alas! that demon of perversity, which visits me at the decisive moment when I ought to act, wished things otherwise, and brought about the clumsy abortion of this lovely project. At the dinner which was to seal this quite Parisian union, I behaved in so unmannerly a fashion to the young woman that after a scandalous scene she left the salon in shame, fury and tears, and went home, widowed of both our loves. The little celebration was cut short, and Eugene took me home in a cab. We went down the Champs Elysees amid a tragic silence.

"Where shall I drop you off?" the great man said to me, as we turned the corner of the Rue Royale.

"At the dive... on the boulevard," I sneeringly replied to them, in a hurry to breathe some pure air, in the company of honest people. And suddenly, with a gesture of discouragement, my friend tapped me on the knee and oh, all my life I shall see the sinister expression of his mouth, and his look of hatred!——and he sighed:

"Well! Well! No good will ever come of you!"

He was right. And that time I could not blame him for it.

Eugene Mortain belonged to that school of politicians which, under the famous name of opportunists, Gambetta unleashed upon France like a pack of carnivorous beasts. He aspired to power only for the material pleasures it could procure, and the money which clever men like he knew how to draw from muddy sources. Incidentally, I do not know why I am holding only Gambetta responsible for the historic honor of having gathered and unchained the miserable pack which still endures despite all the Panamas. Gambetta assuredly loved corruption; there lay in that thundering democrat a voluptuary, or rather a lusty dilettante who reveled in the stench of decomposition. But it must be said in his exoneration, and to their glory, that the friends with whom he surrounded himself, and which chance rather than judicious selection had rallied to his short-lived career, were rascals enough to hurl themselves of their own accord, upon that eternal prey, in which so very many jaws had already fleshed their furious teeth.

Before attaining to the Chamber, Eugene Mortain had tackled every trade—even the lowest; he had passed through the lowest and shadiest depths of journalism, You cannot choose all your openings—you must take them where you find them. His initiation into Parisian life was spirited and prompt—and, moreover, carefully calculated. I mean that life which flows from the editorial offices to the Parliament, by way of the prefecture of police. Since he was devoured by immediate needs and ruinous appetites, there was no important blackmailing scheme or underhand affair of which our honest Eugene was not in some way or other the mysterious and violent brain. He had negotiated that stroke of genius whereby a great section of the press had been syndicated, in order to expedite the success of his vast undertakings. In this sort of discredited enterprise knew a good many of his calculations to be pure master-pieces, which revealed this little, rapidly cultivated provincial as an astounding psychologist and an admirable organizer of the evil instincts of the outcast. But he had the modesty never to boast of the beauty of his achievements, and the priceless art, by making use of others, of never exposing his own person in hours of danger. With constant craftiness and a perfect knowledge of his fields of operation, he always managed to avoid, by circumnavigation, the dank and muddy swamps of the police correctional, into which so many others clumsily allowed themselves to be engulfed. It is true that my assistance—be it said without fatuity—was not entirely useless to him in many circumstances. He was, into the bargain, a charming fellow; yes, in truth, a charming fellow. He could only be reproached for an awkwardness of demeanor—a persistent vestige of his provincial education—and vulgar details which added to the unpleasant conspicuousness of his too recently acquired wealth. But all these things were only externals which concealed all the better, from casual observers, whatever subtle resources his mind possessed, together with his acute instincts, his shrewd agility, and all the greedy and terrible tenacity of his soul. To rightly appreciate that soul it would have been necessary to see—as I, alas, have seen them so many times!—the two wrinkles which, at certain moments of relaxation, drooped from the corners of his lips and gave a frightful expression to his mouth—Ah yes, he was a charming fellow!

"By judicious duels he silenced the malevolent rumors which always surround meteoric personalities. His natural gaiety and good—natured cynicism (which we readily considered an amiable paradox), no less than his lucrative and widely pub-licized love-affairs, succeeded in acquiring for him a questionable reputation, which was, however, enough for a future statesman who Was yet to go through the mill. He also possessed that marvelous faculty of being able to speak for five hours and on any subject, without ever expressing an idea. His quenchless elo-quence poured forth ceaseless and indefatigable—the slow, monotonous, and sui-cidal torrent of the political vocabulary—and just as fluently upon questions of the merchant marine as on school reform, on finance as well as the beaux arts, on agriculture as well as religion. The parliamentary reporters recognized in him their own universal incompetence, and patterned their written jargon after his spo-ken gibberish. Obliging when it cost him nothing; generous and even prodigal when it might be very profitable to him; arrogant and servile according to circum-stances and individuals; awkwardly skeptical, grossly corrupt, an enthusiast devoid of spontaneity and an unspontaneous wit—he was liked by everyone. Therefore his swift rise surprised and disconcerted no one. It was, to the contrary, favorably received by different political parties, for Eugene was not considered a fierce partisan, he discouraged no hope or ambition, and it was not unknown that, when the time was ripe, an understanding might be reached with him. All that mattered was to set the price. Such was the man and such the 'charming fellow' in whom my last hopes rested, and who actually held my life and death between his fingers.

You will notice that in this hastily outlined sketch of my friend I have modestly effaced myself, although I collaborated vigorously, and often by curious methods, in the making of his career. I might tell any number of stories which are not, you may believe, exceptionally edifying. But what good would a complete confession be, since you may guess at all my depravities without any necessity for further display? And then, my role opposite this bold and prudent scamp was always—I do not say insignificant, ah nor laudable, for you would laugh in my face—but it remained almost a secret. Allow me to remain in that scarcely discreet shadow with which I have been pleased to shroud those years of sinister struggle and shady machination. Eugene does not 'acknowledge' me. And I myself, out of what remains of a quite bizarre modesty, occasionally feel an overwhelming repugnance at the thought that I might easily pass for his 'cat's-paw'.

Besides, it occasionally happened that for entire months I lost sight of him, and 'gave him the slip', as we say, finding in the gambling-dens, at the Stock Exchange and in the dressing-rooms of kept women, sustenance which I was tired of seeking in politics, and whose quest was more to my taste for laziness and the unexpected. Sometimes, in the grip of a sudden poetic mood, I buried myself in a God-forsaken corner of the country, and in the presence of nature aspired to purity, silence and moral rehabilitation which, alas! never lasted very long. And I returned to Eugene at times of crisis. He did not always welcome me with the cordiality I demanded of him. It was obvious that he would have liked to get rid of me. But with a clean, sharp cut of the check-rein, I recalled him to the reality of our mutual situation.

One day I distinctly saw the flame of murder glowing in his eyes. I was not alarmed, but firmly placed my hand upon his shoulder, like a gendarme does to a robber, and I said banteringly:

"What of it? What will it get you? My corpse itself will accuse you. Don't be so stupid! I've let you get where you wanted. I've never crossed your ambition. To the contrary, I have worked for you as well as I was able... loyally, isn't it true? Do you think it's pleasant for me to see us—you on top, strutting in the limelight, and me at the bottom, stupidly floundering through the mire? And then, by a flip of the hand, this marvelous career, laboriously built up by us both—"

"Oh! by us both... " hissed Eugene.

"Yes, by us both, swine!" I repeated, exasperated by this untimely correction. "Yes, by a flip of the hand... a breath... and you know it—I could destroy that marvelous career. I need only say one word, you cur, to hurl you from power to the workhouse; to make of the Minister you are—ah, so ironically!—the galley slave you might be if justice still existed and I weren't the basest of cowards. Well! I will not make that gesture, and I won't say the word. I leave you to receive the adulation of men and the esteem of foreign courts, because, you see... I find it stupendously amusing. Only, I want my share, you hear!... my share. And what do I ask? What I ask is ridiculous. Nothing—crumbs... although I might demand everything—everything! I beg you—don't exasperate me any further; don't drive me to the wall any longer. Don't force me to create melodramatic scenes. For the day I have had enough of life, enough, of the slime, that slime—your slime, whose intolerable odor I smell about me all the time... well, that day his Excellency Eugene Mortain won't laugh, my boy. I swear it!"

Then, with an embarrassed smile, in which the folds around his drooping lips gave his face an expression of beastly fear and impotent lust to kill, Eugene said to me:

"But you're crazy to tell me all this... and apropos of what? Have I refused you anything, you sorehead?"

And, gaily, with a multiplicity of gesture and grimace which bewildered me, he comically added;

"Do you want the Cross of the Legion of Honor, eh?"

Yes, truly, he was a charming fellow.

PART 3

Some days after the scene of violence which followed my unfortunate defeat I met Eugene again at a friend's house, the home of that good Mme. G—, where we had both been invited to dine. Our handshake was cordial and you'd have thought nothing unpleasant had passed between us.

"I don't see you anymore," he reproached me, in that tone of noncommittal geniality which in him was only the refinement of hatred. "Have you been ill?"

"Certainly not. I travel towards oblivion, that's all."

"Incidentally—have you recovered your senses? I'd like very much to talk to you for five minutes after dinner... if you don't mind."

"Then you've got something new?" I asked with a bitter smile, so he might see that I refused to be dismissed as a matter of little consequence.

"I?" he said. "No... nothing... a tentative project. Well, we'll see."

I was ready with an impertinent reply when Mme. G—, an enormous bundle of swaying flowers, dancing feathers and billowing lace, interrupted our conversation. "Ah, my dear Minister," she sighed, "when will you ever rid us of these dreadful socialists?" And she carried Eugene off to a group of young women who, by the way they were grouped in a corner of the salon, impressed me with being there for hire, like those nocturnal creatures at a cafe-concert who, with their excessive décolletage and borrowed finery, add the final touch to their tawdry surroundings.

Mme. G— had the reputation of playing an important part in Society and the Government, and among the innumerable comedies of Parisian life, the influence attributed to her was not one of the least amusing. The paltry chroniclers of the petty events of that time seriously related (after establishing brilliant parallels in the past), that her salon was the starting-point and the goal of political careers and literary aspirations; and consequently the rendezvous of all the young and ambitious, and the old and likewise. According to them, it was there that contemporary history was made, there the downfall and accession of cabinets was plotted, and there, amid genial intrigues and delicious small-talk, for it was a salon where people talked—that foreign alliances as well as academic elections were negotiated. It was said that M. Sadi Carnot himself—who then reigned over French hearts—had been given to clever maneuvers in his dealings with this formidable power, and to keep in its good graces he gallantly offered it, for lack of his approbation, the most beautiful flowers of the Elysee gardens and the city hothouses. From having known M. Thiers and M. Guizot, Cavour and the elder Metternich, during the time of her, or their youth—Mme. G— was not very sure of her chronology on that point—this ancient personage retained a prestige with which the Republic loved to adorn itself, as with a perennial grace; and her salon benefited by the posthumous glory which those illustrious names (invoked on all occasions) recalled to the shrunken individualities of the present.

Moreover, people went to this select salon as to a county fair; and never have I seen—I who've seen so many a stranger medley of human beings or a more ridiculous social masquerade. There was a host of out casts from the worlds of politics, journalism, clubs, society, the theatre and the world at large—and women of the same sort—she received them all. No one was deceived by this pseudo-atmosphere, but each one found it incumbent—in order to exalt himself—to glorify a notoriously low environment in which many of us found, not only scarcely mentionable sustenance, but even our only reason for being. Besides, I have an idea that most of the salons so famous in former times where roving political ambitions and unemployed literary pretensions of the most varied species came to commune, resembled this one pretty accurately... No more am I convinced that this one differed essentially from others highly praised in lyrical panegyrics and on all occasions, for their difficulty of access or their exquisite moral standards.

The truth is that Mme. G—, stripped of her exaggerated fame and poetic legends and reduced to the real character of her worldly personality, was just a very vulgar-minded old woman, of scant and, in the bargain extremely vicious education. No longer able to cultivate the flower of vice in her own garden, she cultivated it elsewhere with a tranquil shamelessness. It was difficult to know whether its boldness or its ingenuousness was more to be admired. For professional love-affairs, which she had been obliged to abandon, she had substituted a mania for contriving extramarital unions and separations, which it was her delight and her only sin to follow up, direct, protect and hatch; and thus warm her shriveled old heart by the heat of their forbidden flames. At the home of this great politician, sanctified by Messieurs Thiers and Guizot, by Cavour and the elder Metternich, you were always sure to find kindred souls, impending adultery, lusts under weigh, and passions of all kinds, freshly equipped for the race at any time an invaluable stock-in-trade in the event of sentimental ruptures and dull evenings.

Why did I have the idea of going to Mme. G—'s that particular evening? I don't know, for I was quite melancholy and scarcely in the mood for merrymaking. My anger with Eugene was quite appeased, at least momentarily, and a great fatigue—a great disgust, had replaced it: disgust with myself, with others, with everybody. Since that morning I had reflected seriously on my situation, and despite the Minister's promises with which, moreover, I had decided not to let him off easily—I saw no suitable outcome. I realized that it was quite difficult for my friend to procure me a permanent official situation, something honorably parasitical and officially remunerative, by whose means I might be enabled to end my days in peace—a respectable old man and an irreproachable office-holder. Besides, it is probable that I would have immediately bungled this position; then, from all sides, simultaneous objections would have been raised in the name of public morality and the decency of the Republic, to which the Minister, when questioned, would not have known how to reply. Anything he could offer me through transitory and miserable expedients and sorry juggling of the budget, would only have been a postponement of the inevitable hour of my downfall. And then I could not even count on this minimum of favors and protection forever, any more than Eugene could count upon the everlasting stupidity of the public. Many dangers already threatened the cabinet, and many scandals, to which, now and then, some newspapers, dissatisfied with the graft they were receiving, were making more and more direct allusions and undermining the personal security of my protector, Eugene only maintained his power by aggressive attacks upon unpopular and defeated parties, and also by cash payments which, as I suspected at the time, and was later demonstrated, he received from outside, in exchange each time for a pound of the country's flesh.

I had carefully considered working for the downfall of my comrade, and cleverly worming my way to the side of a likely ministerial leader, and thus, by the aid of this new collaborator, recovering a sort of social virginity. Everything impelled me to it: my nature, my own welfare, and also the violently delicious pleasure of vengeance. But besides the uncertainties and dangers which surrounded this scheme, I had neither the courage to risk another adventure, nor to repeat such maneuvers. I had burned my candle at both ends, and I was weary of these perilous and precarious adventures which had led me—whither? I was experiencing mental fatigue, a paralysis of my energies, and all my faculties were diminishing while still in their prime, sapped by neurasthenia. Ah, how I regretted not having followed the straight roads of life! At the moment I sincerely hope for nothing better than the mediocre joys of middle-class respectability, and I wished no more, and could bear no more of these sudden jolts of fortune, these choices of misery which had not left me a moment of respite, and had made of my existence a perpetual and tortured anxiety. Then what was to become of me? The future seemed sadder and even more hopeless to me than winter twilight falling in a sickroom. In a little while, after dinner, what new infamy would the infamous Minister propose to me? Into what deeper mire, from which I could never rise, did he want to thrust me, and make me disappear forever?

I glanced about for him amid the throng. He was hovering about the women. Nothing about his skull or shoulders indicated that he bore the heavy burden of his crimes. He was carefree and gay. And to see him thus redoubled my rage at the realization of our mutual impotence—his to save me from shame, and mine to fling him into it... ah yes, to fling him into it!

Crushed by these multiple, piercing preoccupations, it was not astounding that I had lost my fervor, and that the beautiful creatures selected and displayed by Mme. G— for the pleasure of her guests, left me cold.

During dinner I behaved in an extremely disagreeable fashion, and scarcely spoke to my neighbors whose lovely bosoms gleamed amidst their flowers and jewels. It was believed that my electoral defeat was the cause of this somber mood in one so ordinarily joyful and gallant. "Cheer up!" they said to me. "What the devil, you're still young! You need guts for a political career. Better luck next time." To these banal consolations, engaging smiles, and inviting bosoms, I obstinately replied:

"No... no. Don't talk politics to me. It's infamous! Don't talk to me any more about universal suffrage. It's idiotic! I've had enough. I don't want to hear them mentioned again."

Then Mme. G——, her feathers, flowers and lace suddenly rising before me in variegated and scented waves whispered in my ear with the affected raptures and moist coquetries of an old procuress:

"Love is everything, you see. There is never anything but love! Try love! Listen: just tonight there is a young Romanian here... passionate... ah, a poet, my dear, and a countess! I'm sure she's mad about you. Anyhow, all women are mad about you. I'll introduce you."

I side-stepped this crudely arranged opportunity, and in a sullen and enervated silence persistently awaited the end of this interminable evening.

Monopolized by everyone, it was quite late before Eugene could rejoin me. We took advantage of the fact that a celebrated diva was momentarily absorbing everyone's attention, to hide in a sort of little smoking-room which was lit by the discreet glow of a tall floor lamp, draped with rose-colored gauze. The Minister sat down on the couch, lit a cigarette, and while I negligently straddled a chair opposite him and crossed my arms on its back, he seriously said:

"I've been thinking a lot about you these last few days."

Doubtless he expected some word of thanks, a friendly gesture, or a movement which might indicate interest or curiosity. I remained motionless, forcing myself to preserve that air of haughty and almost insolent indifference, with which I had determined to receive the treacherous suggestions of my friend; for, from the beginning of the evening, I had set my heart on these suggestions being treacherous. Insolently, I pretended to look at the portrait of M. Thiers which occupied the top of the panel behind Eugene and was overcast by all the dark shadows which played across its over-varnished surface, with the exception, however, of his white pear shaped topknot which became of itself the unique and complete expression of the obliterated face. Muffled by the closed portieres, the sound of the party came to us like a distant hum. Shaking his head, the Minister went on:

"Yes, I've thought of you a great deal. Well! it's difficult... quite difficult." Again he grew silent, seeming to reflect on important matters.

I took pleasure in prolonging the silence in order to enjoy the embarrassment into which this teasing attitude could not fail to throw my friend. Once more I was to see this dear protector before me, ridiculous and unmasked—perhaps suppliant! He remained calm, however, and did not seem to be in the least concerned with the over—obvious hostility of my bearing.

"You don't believe me," he said, in a firm and tranquil voice. "Yes, I feel you don't believe me. You imagine I only think of fooling you, as I fool the others—isn't that true? Well, you're wrong, my boy. Besides, if this conversation bores you—it's easy enough to break it off." He pretended to get up.

"I didn't say that!" I protested, shifting my glance from M. Thiers' topknot to Eugene's icy face. "I didn't say anything."

"Then listen to me. Shall we talk, once and for all, and in all frankness, about our mutual situation?"

"So be it! I'm listening."

Faced with his assurance, little by little I lost my own. Contrary to what I had so egotistically conjectured Eugene was regaining all his authority over me, and I felt him escaping me again. I felt it by that ease of gesture, that almost elegant manner, that firmness of tone and that entire self-possession which he never really ly displayed except when he was considering his most sinister strokes. At those times he possessed a sort of forceful seductiveness, a magnetic power which it was difficult to resist, even though you were forewarned, Though I knew him, yet to my misfortune I had often been the victim of his malefic charm, which should never have surprised me again. Well! all my belligerence abandoned me, my hatred relaxed, and despite myself I found I was regaining confidence and so completely forgetting the past, that this man whose inexorable and fetid soul I had tracked to its darkest recesses—I discovered I was considering once more a generous friend, a hero of magnanimity—a savior!

Ah, I would like the power to express the accent of force, crime, callousness and ease which he put into his words—and this is what he said to me:

"You've seen politics close enough to know that a degree of power exists at which the most infamous man finds himself protected from himself by his own infamy; and even more strongly, against others, by the infamy of others. There is only one trait which is irreparable in a statesman: honesty! Honesty is negative and sterile; it is ignorant of the correct evaluation of appetite and ambition—the only powers through which you can found anything durable. The proof of this is that idiot Favrot—the only honest man in the Cabinet, and also the only one whose political career is, by common consent, totally and forever lost! Just to let you know, my boy, that a campaign directed against me leaves me absolutely indifferent."

I made a rapid, ambiguous gesture:

"Yes—yes... I know... they're talking about my ruin... my impending, downfall... the police.. the Mazas prison! 'Death to the robbers!' Absolutely! What don't they talk about? Well then? It makes me laugh, that's all! And you yourself, under pretext that you think you've been mixed up in some of my affairs of which, let me say in passing, you know only one side—under pretext of withholding—at least, you go shouting it all over—some vague papers about which, my boy, I give that!"

Without interrupting himself, he showed me his extinguished cigarette, which he immediately crushed in an ashtray that lay on the little lacquer table beside him.

"You yourself... you think you can terrify me into compliance... blackmail me like an insolvent banker! You're a child! Think a minute. My downfall? Now, can you tell me who would dare, at this time, to assume the responsibility for such a piece of insanity?

Who doesn't know that it would involve the cave-in of too many things; too many men whom it is no more possible to reach than I—under penalty of abdication or death? For I wouldn't be the only one to be overthrown. I wouldn't be the only one to wear the ball and chain. The entire Government, the entire Parliament, the entire Republic, whatever it may do, is linked up with what are called my transgressions, my embezzlements, my crimes. They think they've got me, and it's I who have them! Don't worry, I've got a good grip on them." And he clutched an imaginary throat.

The expression of his mouth, with its drooping corners, became hideous, and purple veinlets appeared in his eyeballs, which gave to his glance an implacable suggestion of murder. But he hastily composed himself, lit another cigarette, and went on:

"Let them overthrow the Cabinet—agreed! And I'll help in it. Thanks to the work of that honest Favrot, we're involved in a series of inextricable problem; whose logical solution is simply that they cannot possibly have any. A ministerial crisis is imminent, and an entirely new program. Please notice that I am, or at least I appear to be, alien to these difficulties. My responsibility is only a parliamentary fiction. In the hallways of the Chamber and in certain sections of the press, I am being adroitly separated from my colleagues. Thus, my personal situation of course remains politically clear. Better than that, upheld by the groups whose leaders I've succeeded in interesting in my career, sustained by the big banks and the great companies, I am becoming the one man indispensable to the new regime. I am the chosen President of the forthcoming Council. And it's ate the very moment when my downfall is proclaimed from all sides that I am attaining the peak of my career! I admit that it's comical, my boy, and that they haven't got hold of my hide yet."

Eugene had become sprightly again. The idea that there was no intermediate point for him between these two poles: the Presidency of the Council or the Mazas prison, exhilarated his spirits. He drew close to me and tapping me on the knee, as he did in moments of relaxation or gaiety, he repeated:

"Come... admit it's funny!"

"Very funny!" I agreed. "But what place have I in all this?"

"You? Well, here it is! You, my friend—must go away—disappear... a year... two years... what's that? You need to be forgotten." And as I prepared to object: "But damn it all! Is it my fault?" Eugene cried, "If you've stupidly spoiled all the excellent jobs I've laid in your lap? A year—two years—it's soon over. You'll come back with a new virginity and I'll give you everything you want. Till then, nothing—I can do nothing. My word of honor! I can't do a thing."

I was still somewhat furious, but it was in a weak voice that, I cried: "Damn! damn! damn!" Eugene smiled, realizing that my resistance had ended with that outburst.

"Come, come!" he said to me good-naturedly, "don't be obstinate. Listen to me. I've thought about it a good deal. You must go away. In your interest, for your future. I can't think of anything else. Come! Are you... how shall I put it? Are you an embryologist?" He read my reply in the bewildered look I cast him.

"No! you are no embryologist. Sad! very sad!"

"Why do you ask that? Now what kind of a joke is it?"

"Just this—that at this time I might easily obtain considerable funds—oh, relatively!—but at least substantial funds, for a scientific expedition they might be willing to entrust to you." And without giving me time to reply, in short, humorous sentences accompanied by comical gestures he explained the business to me:

"It involves going to India, Ceylon, I believe, to drag the sea, in the gulfs, and study what the scientists call the pelagic ooze, you understand? And among the gastropoda, the corals, the heteropoda, the madrepora, the siphonophora, the holothuroidea and radiolaria—how should I know?—to discover the primordial cell—pay close attention... the protoplasmic initum of organized life, or something like that. It's charming and as you see—very simple."

"Very simple indeed," I murmured mechanically.

"Yes, but there it is," concluded this true statesman, "you aren't an embryologist." And with benevolent sorrow he added:

"It's annoying!"

My protector reflected a few moments. I was silent, not having had time to recover from the stupor into which this unexpected proposition had plunged me.

"My God!" he went on, "there might be another expedition—for we actually have lots of expeditions and don't know what to spend the donor's money on. If I remember rightly, this one would be to go to the Fiji Islands and Tasmania, to study the various systems of penitentiary administration in use there, and their application to our social system. Only it's less amusing and I must warn you the funds are not enormous. And they're still cannibals down there, you know! You think I'm joking, eh? That I'm telling you a fairytale? But, my boy, all expeditions are like that. Ha!" Eugene started to laugh with gentle malice.

"There is still the secret police. Ha ha! You might possibly find a good job in that... what do you say?"

In difficult circumstances my mental faculties become active and more acute, my energies are unleashed and I am endowed with a sudden influx of ideas, and a promptness of decision which always astonishes me and has often served me well.

"Bah!" I cried, "after all I could easily be an embryologist once in my life. What do I risk? Science won't die of it. It's been through the mill! Done! I accept the expedition to Ceylon."

"And you're right. Bravo!" applauded the Minister; "seeing that embryology, my boy, Darwin, Haeckel... Carl Vogt, after all—it must be a great joke! Ah, my lad you won't be bored down there. Ceylon is marvelous. They say there are extraor-

dinary women there, little lace makers—beautiful—temperamental! It's the earthly paradise! Come to the Ministry tomorrow and we'll wind up the business officially. In the meantime you don't have to shout it from the housetops, because you
know I'm playing a dangerous joke which might cost me dearly. Come!"

We arose and, while I went back to the salon on the Minister's arm, he said again,
with charming irony:

"Eh? After all! Suppose you discover the cell? Who knows? Berthelot would
make a face, eh?"

This scheme had given me back a little courage and a little gaiety. Not that it
pleased me entirely; I would have preferred a general receivership, for instance,
to this commission as an illustrious embryologist, or a well-upholstered seat in the
State's Council. But you have to compromise, and besides, the adventure was not
without its amusing aspect. From a simple political vagabond, such as I had been
a few moments before, you cannot, by a wave of the ministerial wand, become an
eminent scientist about to violate the mysteries at the very springs of life, without
experiencing something of a mystifying pride and a comical grandeur.

The soiree, begun miserably, was ending in hilarity.

I accosted Mme. G—, who was excitedly organizing love, and promenading
adultery from group to group and couple to couple.

"And that adorable Romanian countess," I asked her, ""is she still mad about
me?"

"Still, my dear..."

She took me by the arm. Her feathers were drooping, her flowers wilted, and her
flounces hung limply.

"Come along!" she said; "she's in the little Guizot salon, flirting with Princess
Onane."

"What! she too?"

"But my dear," replied this great politician, "at her age, and with her poetic
nature, it would really be unfortunate if she had not tried everything!"

PART 4

My preparations were soon made. I was lucky in that the young Romanian countess, who had become quite attached to me, was willing to assist me with her
advice and, I say it with shame—with her purse too.

Besides I had all the luck. My expedition got off to a good start. By an exceptional anomaly of bureaucratic procedure, eight days after that conclusive conversation in Mme. G—'s salons, I obtained the above-mentioned funds without the
slightest red tape or delay. They were more generously computed than I had dared
to hope, for I was familiar with the swinishness of the government in these matters, and the poor little arbitrary budgets by which they so pitifully gratify scientists on expeditions—real scientists. Undoubtedly, lowed this unusual liberality
the fact that, not being a scientist at all, I had more need than anyone else for
greater resources, in order to play the part.

They had counted on the maintenance of two secretaries and two servants, the costly purchase of anatomical instruments, microscopes, photographic apparatus, collapsible boats, diving-bells, and even wide-mouthed jars for scientific collections, hunting rifles and cages designed to bring captured animals back alive. Truly, the government does things in grand style, and I could not help but praise it. It goes without saying that I did not buy any of these *impedimenta,* and that I decided not to take anyone along, counting upon my ingenuity alone to find my way in the midst of these untracked jungles of science and India.

I profited by my leisure to inform myself about Ceylon, its customs and landscapes, and to construct an idea of the life I would lead down there in those terrible tropics. Even after eliminating the exaggerated, boastful, and mendacious elements of travelers' tales, I was enchanted by what I read—particularly by this detail, reported by a sober German savant: that in the suburbs of Colombo there exists, amid fairy gardens by the sea, a marvelous villa bungalow, as they say, in which a rich and eccentric Englishman maintains a sort of harem, where all the races of India, from the black Tamoules to the sinuous bayaderes of Lahore, and the demoniac bacchantes of Benares, are represented by perfect specimens of femininity. I definitely made up my mind to find some means of gaining access to this amateur polygamist, and to confine my studies of comparative embryology to that spot.

The Minister, whom I visited to say goodbye and confide my plans, approved all these projects, and quite gaily praised the virtue of my economy. When he left me he spoke with an emotional eloquence, while I, under the torrent of his words, experienced a tenderness—the pure, refreshing and sublime tenderness of a good man.

"Go, my friend, and come back to us stronger... come back to us a new man and a glorious savant. Your exile, which I have no doubt you will employ in the accomplishment of great deeds, will replenish your energies for future struggles. It will temper them in the very springs of life, in the cradle of humanity which... of humanity, of which... Go... and if on your return you find—which I cannot believe—if you can, I say, bad memories persisting, difficulties... hostility... an obstacle to your rightful ambitions... remember that you possess enough little memoranda about the governmental personnel to triumph over it with a high hand. *Sursum corda!* Count on me, besides. While you are down there, courageous pioneer of progress and a soldier of science... while you are sounding the gulfs and questing the mysterious atolls for France, for our dear France—I shan't forget you, you may well believe me. Cleverly, step by step, through the *Agence Havas* and in my own newspapers, I shall find a means of creating a commotion about you—our coming young embryologist. I'll devise magnificent and pathetic blurbs—'Our great embryologist'... 'We learn from our young and illustrious savant, whose embryological discoveries, etc.'... 'While he was studying a hitherto unknown holoihurian under twenty fathoms of water, our indefatigable embryologist barely escaped being carried off by a shark... a terrific struggle... etc.' Go, go, my friend, work fearlessly for the glory of the nation. Today a race is not only treat by virtue of its arms; it is great, above all, through its arts... through its sciences. The peaceful conquests of science serve civilization more than the conquests of... etc., etc... *Cedant arma sapientio!"*

I wept for joy, pride, grandeur and exaltation—the exaltation of my being towards something stupendous, and stupendously beautiful. Projected beyond my ego, I know not whence, I had, at that moment, another soul—an almost divine soul, a creative and sacrificial soul—the soul of some sublime hero in whom the supreme confidence of the nation resides—and all the strongest hopes of humanity.

As for the Minister—that bandit Eugene—he could scarcely contain his emotion. He had real enthusiasm in his glance, a sincere quaver in his voice. Two little tears fell from his eyes. He almost crushed my hand in his grip. For several moments both of us were the unconscious and comic toys of our own deception.

Ah, when I think of it!

PART 5

Armed with letters of Recommendation to the authorities at Ceylon, I finally embarked at Marseille one splendid afternoon, on the *Saghalien.*

From the moment I set foot on the steamer, I was immediately aware of the value of an official title, and how, by the prestige which attaches to it, a fallen man, such as I was then, rises in the estimation of unknown people and passersby, and consequently in his own. The captain, who 'knew my works', overwhelmed me with attentions—almost with honors. The most comfortable cabin had been reserved for me, and also the best place at table. As the news had rapidly spread among the passengers of the presence on board of a celebrated scientist, everyone went out of his way to pay me his respects. I saw nothing but a glow of admiration on their faces. The women themselves gave evidence of curiosity and good will; some, discreetly, and others, by manifesting a bolder sentiment. One, above all, violently attracted my attention. She was a marvelous creature with heavy copper hair and green eyes flecked with gold, like those of jungle beasts. She was traveling with three maids—one of whom was Chinese. I inquired about her from the captain.

"She's English," he said to me, "they call her Miss Clara. The most extraordinary woman on earth. Although she's only twenty-eight years old, she's been all over the world already. Just now she lives in China. This is the fourth time I've seen her aboard."

"Rich?"

"Oh, very rich! They tell me her father, who's been dead a long time, was an opium dealer in Canton. That's where she was born, in fact. She's a little cracked, I think, but charming."

"Married?"

"No."

"And?"

Into that conjunction I put a whole battalion of intimate and even impertinent questions. The captain smiled.

"That I can't say. I don't think so. I've never noticed anything—here."

Such was the reply of the good mariner who, it seemed to me, knew a good deal more about it than he wished to say. I did not insist, but I said to myself:

"You, my girl... absolutely!"

The first passengers with whom I became acquainted were two Chinese of the London Embassy and a Norman gentleman who was on his way to Tonkin. The latter was immediately quite willing to confide in me. He was an ardent hunter.

"I'm running away from France," he told me. "I escape every time I can. Since we've become a republic, France is a lost country. There are too many poachers, and they're the masters. Would you believe that I can't keep any game on my place any more! The poachers kill it for me, and the courts uphold them. It's a bit too much! Without counting the fact that the few they leave croak of God knows what epidemics. So I'm going to Tonkin. What a fine hunting-ground! It's the fourth time, my dear sir, that I'm going to Tonkin."

"Ah, really?"

"Yes! In Tonkin every sort of game is abundant. But especially the peacock. What shooting, sir! Besides, it's a dangerous sport; you have to have an eye for it." "Doubtless these are ferocious peacocks?"

"My God, no. But this is the way it is: Wherever there are deer, there are tigers... and wherever there are tigers, there are peacocks!"

"An aphorism?"

"You must understand me. Follow carefully... the tiger eats the deer, and—"

"The peacock eats the tiger?" I gravely suggested. "Absolutely... that is to say... here is the thing. When the tiger is gorged with the deer, 'he falls asleep; then he awakes, relieves himself and goes away. What does the peacock do? Perched in the neighboring trees, he prudently awaits this departure, then he drops to earth and eats the tiger's dung. And that is the precise moment you must surprise him... " And with his arms raised as though holding a rifle, he made the gesture of ,aiming at an imaginary peacock:

"Ah, what peacocks! you haven't the least idea! For, what you take for peacocks in our aviaries and gardens, aren't even turkeys. They're nothing. My dear sir, I've killed all sorts of things. I've even killed men. Well! never has the report of a rifle given me so keen an emotion as the times I've fire at peacocks. Peacocks, how can I tell you, sir... are *magnificent* to kill!" Then, after a silence, he concluded:

"Travel—that's the thing! In traveling you see extraordinary things which make you think."

"Doubtless," I agreed, "but one must be a great observer, like you."

"It's true! I've observed a great deal," the good gentleman ostentatiously said. "Well, of all the countries I've traveled in—Japan, China; Madagascar, Haiti, and a section of Australia—I know none more entertaining than Tonkin. Now perhaps you think you've seen hens?"

"Yes, I believe so—"

"Your error, my dear sir, you have never seen hens. You have to go to Tonkin for that, and then you won't see them. They're in the forests, and they hide in the trees. You never see them. Only, I have a trick. I travel upstream in a sampan, with a cock in a cage. I stop at the edge of the forest and hang the cage at the end of a branch. The cock crows. Then from all the depths of the forest, the hens come... and come. They come in unnumbered bands. And I kill them! I have killed as many as twelve hundred in the same day!"

"It's remarkable!" I exclaimed enthusiastically.

"Yes, yes. But not as much so as peacocks, however. Ah, the peacocks!"

But this gentleman was not only a hunter; he was also a gambler. Long before we were in sight of Naples, the two Chinese, the peacock-killer and I had gotten up a fast game of poker. Thanks to my special knowledge of that game, when we arrived at Port Said, I had relieved these three incomparable gentlemen of their money and tripled the capital I was bearing toward the joys of the tropics, and the Unknown of fictitious embryology.

PART 6

At that time I would have been incapable of the meagerest poetical description—poetry having come to me afterwards, with love. To be sure, I enjoyed the beauties of nature, like everybody else, but they had never overwhelmed me to the point of ecstasy; I enjoyed them, in my way, which was that of a conservative republican. And I said to myself:

"Nature, seen from a train window or the porthole of a ship, is always and everywhere herself; her principal characteristic being that she lacks the ability for improvisation. She repeats herself constantly, possessing but a small stock of forms, combinations and aspects, which are found here and there in almost identical arrangements. In her immense and clumsy monotony, she varies only in scarcely perceptible nuances, which are only interesting to trainers of little animals, which I am not—though an embryologist—and to splitters of hairs. Briefly, when you have traveled over a hundred square miles of countryside, no matter where, you have seen everything." And that little swine Eugene had exclaimed:

"You'll see nature... trees... flowers!"

As far as I'm concerned, trees get on my nerves, and I only tolerate flowers in the modiste's shops, and on hats. As for tropical nature—Monte Carlo would have been amply sufficient to my needs as an esthetic connoisseur of landscapes, and my dreams of distant travel. I understand palm trees, cocoanuts, bananas, mangroves, shaddock and pandanus, only if I can gather in their shade all sorts of pretty little women who munch between their lips something better than the betel-nut. Coconut tree: the cocotte-tree. I only like trees of this truly Parisian classification.

Ah, what a deaf and blind brute I was then! How could I, with such nauseating cynicism, have blasphemed the infinite beauty of Form, which passes from man to beast, from beast to plant, from the plant to the mountain, the mountain to the cloud, and from the cloud to the pebble, which contains in reflection all the splendors of life!

Although it was the month of October, the crossing of the Red Sea was excruciating. The heat was crushing, and the air so heavy on our European lungs that many times I thought I would die of asphyxiation. During the day we scarcely left the saloon where the great Indian *punka,* constantly in motion, gave us the evanescent illusion of a fresh breeze; and we passed the nights on the deck where, however, it was no more possible for us to sleep than in our cabins. The Norman gentleman panted like an ailing bull, and thought no more of.relating his stories of the hunting in Tonkin. The most boastful and intrepid of the passengers were the most completely knocked out... inert of limb and wheezing like foundered beasts. There was nothing more ridiculous than the sight of these people, prostrate in their variegated pajamas. Only the two Chinese seemed insensible to this flaming temperature; they had changed their behavior no more than their clothes, and spent their time in silent promenades on the deck or playing cards or dice in their cabins.

We couldn't get interested in anything. Besides, nothing distracted us from the torture of feeling ourselves cooking slowly and steadily, like a stew. The steamer was sailing across the gulf: above us, around us, there was nothing but the blue sky and the blue sea—a dark blue—the blue of heated metal here and there reflecting the glow of the forge upon its surface. We could scarcely make out the coasts of Somaliland—that red and distant mass shrouded by the vaporous heat of mountains of burning sand, where no tree or grass grew, and whose shores contained this sinister sea—an immense reservoir of bailing water—in a constantly seething cauldron. I might say that during this crossing I displayed great courage, and succeeded in concealing my actual state of suffering. I attained it through conceit and love.

Chance—was it really chance, or the captain?—had given me Miss Clara for a table-mate. An incident at table brought about our almost immediate acquaintance. Besides, my high station and the curiosity of which I was the object, authorized certain lapses from the ordinary conventions of good breeding.

As I had learned from the captain, Miss Clara was returning to China after dividing her entire summer between England, for her business affairs, Germany for her health, and France for her amusements. She confessed to me that Europe disgusted her more and more. She could no longer endure its provincial customs, its ridiculous habits, and its skimpy landscapes. She only felt happy and free in China. She was of a very resolute demeanor, a very extraordinary mode of life,

talked sometimes at random and sometimes with a lively feeling for things; of a
feverish gaiety pushed to the bizarre, sentimental and philosophic, ignorant and
educated, impure and frank and mysterious. Finally, she was given to strange
lapses, flights of fancy, incomprehensible caprices and terrible desires, and
intrigued me greatly although one must expect everything of an eccentric
Englishwoman. And I never doubted from the start I who, in the matter of women,
had only known—Parisian cocottes—and what is worse, female politicians and
literati—I never doubted that I might easily have conquered this one, and I looked
forward to enjoying my trip with her in an unexpected and charming manner.
With her reddish hair and gleaming skin, a laugh always ready to peal forth from
her fleshy red lips, she was truly the delight of the ship and like its soul was en
route towards mad adventures and the idyllic freedom of virgin countries and the
fiery tropics. The Eve of that marvelous paradise—a flower herself—flower of
intoxication and the tasty fruit of eternal desire, I could see her wander and skip
about amid the flowers and golden fruits of the primordial orchards, no longer in
this dress of white poplin, which molded her lithe form and filled out her bosom
with pulsating life, like a bud, but in the supernatural splendor of her biblical
nudity.

I was not slow to recognize the error of my gallant diagnosis, and the fact that
Miss Clara) contrary to what I had so egotistically predicted, was impregnably
virtuous. Far from being frustrated by this discovery, she appeared all the prettier
to me, and I conceived an actual pride in the fact that she, the pure and virtuous,
accepted me—vile and debauched as I was—with such simple and gracious confidence. I did not want to listen to the inner voices which were crying; 'This
woman lies. This woman is laughing at you. Look, idiot! at those eyes which have
seen everything; that mouth which has kissed everything; those hands which have
caressed very thing; that flesh which has so often trembled with all the lusts, and
in every possible embrace! Pure? Ha! And those knowing gestures? And that softness and suppleness, and those movements of the body which retain all the gestures of the caress? And that bust, swollen like the calyx of a flower drunk with
pollen?' No, in truth, I did not listen to them. And for me it was a deliciously
chaste sensation, compounded of tenderness, gratitude and pride—a sensation of
moral rehabilitation, to enter further every day into an intimacy with a lovely and
virtuous person, whom I decided at the beginning would never be anything to
me—nothing but a soul! This idea elevated me and rehabilitated me in my own
eyes. Thanks to this pure daily contact, I was gaining—yes, gaining self-respect.
All the mire of my past was being transformed to luminous azure, and I glimpsed
the future through the tranquil, limpid emerald of continual happiness. Oh, how
far from me were Eugene Mortain, Mme. G—, and their like! How all those faces
of grinning phantoms were melting by the minute, more and more, beneath the
celestial glance of this lustral creature through whom I was being revealed to
myself as a new man, with generosity, tenderness, and impulses I would never

have expected of myself.

Oh, the ironical tenderness of love! Ah, the comic enthusiasms which lie within the human soul! Often, beside Clara, I believed in the reality and grandeur of my mission, and that I had in me the genius to revolutionize the embryology of the entire universe.

One thing leading to another, we soon arrived at mutual confidences. By a series of cleverly calculated lies which, prompted on one hand by vanity and on the other by a quite natural desire not to lower myself in the mind of my friend, I displayed myself entirely to my advantage in my role of scientist, narrated my biological discoveries, my academic successes, and all the hopes which the most illustrious men of science placed in my theory and my trip. Then, abandoning these somewhat arduous heights, I mixed anecdotes of my social life with appreciations of literature and art, half-sound and half-perverse, enough to interest the mind of a woman without disturbing it. And these light and frivolous conversations to which I forced myself to give a witty turn, endowed my grave scientific personality with a particular and perhaps unique character. I succeeded in conquering Miss Clara during that crossing of the Red Sea. Overcoming my discomfort, I was able to devise ingenious and delicate attentions which assuaged her own discomfort. When the *Saghalien* touched at Aden to take on coal, she and I were perfect friends—friends blessed by that miraculous friendship which is not troubled by a single glance, and whose lovely lucidity is not tarnished by an ambiguous gesture or a guilty design. Still, the voices in me kept crying: 'But look at those nostrils which breathe in all life with terrific lust. Look at those teeth which so often have bitten into the bleeding fruit of sin.' Heroically, I silenced them.

It was a great joy when we entered the waters of the Indian Ocean; after the excruciating and torturing days on the Red Sea, it seemed like a resurrection. A new life, a life of gaiety and activity took possession of the ship, although the temperature was still very warm, the air was delicious to breathe, like the scent of furs that a woman has just laid aside. A light breeze, apparently impregnated with all the perfumes of the tropical flora, refreshed the body and the mind. And all about us there was a dazzling brilliance. The sky, translucid as a fairy grotto, was of a green gold, streaked with rose; the calm sea, heaving with a powerful rhythm under the breath of the monsoon, lay before us extraordinarily blue, and mottled here and there by great emerald-green whorls. We actually felt the physical caress of the approach of magic continents, the lands of light where life, one mysterious day, had uttered its first infantile cries. And on all our faces, even the Norman gentleman's, there was a little of that sky, that sea, and that light.

Miss Clara—it goes without saying—attracted and greatly excited the men; she was always surrounded by a court of passionate adulators. I was not at all jealous, being certain that she considered them all ridiculous, and that she preferred me to all the others, even to the two Chinese with whom she held frequent conversations, but whom she did not look at (as she did me) with that strange look in which I seemed several times, and with great reluctance, to have discovered moral complicity and a secret meaning.

Among the most fervent there was a French explorer who Was going to the Malay Peninsula to study its copper-mines, and an English officer whom we had taken on at Aden, and who was returning to his post at Bombay. They were, each in his own way, heavy but amusing brutes, whom Clara loved to make fun of. The explorer was ceaselessly talking about his recent trek across central Africa. As for the English officer, who was a captain in the artillery, he tried to dazzle Us by describing all his inventions in ballistics.

One evening on deck, after dinner, we were all gathered about Clara, who was delightfully lounging in a rocking-chair. Some smoked cigarettes and others dreamed. All of us, at heart, had this same desire for Clara, and all, with the same dream of ardent possession, followed the play of her little feet clad in their small pink mules, which, with the rocking of the chair, extended from the perfumed calyx of her skirts, like the pistils of a flower. We said nothing. The night was magically balmy and the ship glided voluptuously along on the sea, as though on silk. Clara addressed the explorer:

"Well?" she said, in a malicious voice, "you're not joking? You've actually eaten human flesh?"

"Yes, certainly!" he replied proudly, and in a tone which established his indisputable superiority over us. "We simply had to... you eat what you can get."

"What does it taste like?" she asked, slightly disgusted. He thought a moment. Then making a vague gesture:

"My God!" he said, "how can I explain it? Imagine, adorable lady—imagine pork—pork pickled slightly in nutmeg oil." Careless and resigned, he added:

"It's not very good. Besides, you don't eat it out of gluttony. I prefer a leg of mutton, or a beefsteak."

"Obviously!" consented Clara. And, as though out of politeness she had wished to minimize the horror of this anthropology, she specified:

"Because, undoubtedly, you only ate negro flesh!"

"Negro!" he exclaimed with a start. "Ugh! Luckily, dear lady, I was not driven to that harsh necessity. We never lacked for whites, thank God! Our escort was large, and composed chiefly of Europeans. Marseillais, Germans, Italians... a little of everything. When we were too hungry, we slaughtered one of the escort, preferably a German. The German, divine lady, is fatter than the other races, and he provides more. And then, for us other Frenchmen, it was one German less! The Italian is dry and tough—.full of sinews—"

"And the Marseillais?" I interrupted.

"Ugh!" declared the traveler, tossing his head. "The Marseillais is much too rich; he smells of garlic and also, I don't know why, of grease. I wouldn't say he was appetizing... no... he's edible, that's all." Turning to Clara with gestures of protestation, he insisted:

"But negro flesh—never! I think I would have thrown it up. I know people who have eaten it... they fell sick. The negro is indigestible. There are even some, I assure you, who are poisonous." But, scrupulously, he corrected himself:

"After all, you have to try him once—like mushrooms, eh? Perhaps the Indian negroes allow themselves to be eaten?"

"No!" affirmed the English officer in an abrupt and categorical tone that, in the midst of laughter, closed this culinary discussion which was beginning to turn my stomach.

A little discountenanced, the explorer went on:

"No matter... despite all these slight annoyances, I am very happy to have left again. In Europe I'm sick... I'm not alive... I don't know where to go. In Europe I feel degraded and imprisoned, like a beast in a cage. Impossible to find elbow-room, extend your arms or open your mouth, without bumping into stupid preju-dices and idiotic laws... evil customs. Last year, charming lady, I was walking through a wheat field. I mowed down the blades around me with my cane... it amused me. Surely I have the right to do what pleases me, haven't I? A peasant ran up and started to shout, insult me, order me out of his field. It's unimaginable! What would you have done in my place? I dealt him three vigorous blows on the head with my cane. He fell with a fractured skull. Well, imagine what happened to me—"

"Perhaps you ate him—?" Clara laughingly suggested. "No. They dragged me before some judges or other, who sentenced: me to two months in prison and ten thousand francs fine and damages. For a damned peasant! And they call that civ-ilization! Can you believe it! Well, much obliged—in Africa, if I had been sen-tenced like that every time I'd kill a negro, or even a white—"

"Oh, you've also killed negroes?" said Clara.

"Yes, certainly, adorable lady."

"Why—since you don't eat them?"

"Well—to civilize them—that is to say, to take their stocks of ivory and resins. And then, what do you expect? If the governments and business houses who entrust colonizing expeditions to us learned that we hadn't killed anyone, what would they say?"

"That's true!" agreed the Norman gentleman. "Besides, negroes are wild beasts.—. poachers... tigers.

"Negroes? What a mistake, my dear sir. They are gentle and gay... they are like children. Have you ever seen rabbits playing in the meadow in the evening, at the edge of the woods?"

"Certainly!"

"They make pretty, frolicsome movements; they shine their fur with their paws and bound about and roll in the mint-leaves. Well, negroes are like young rab-bits... it's very charming!"

"However, it *is* certain that they're cannibals?" persisted the gentleman.

"Negroes!" protested the explorer. "Not at all! in all the black Countries the whites are the only cannibals. The negroes eat bananas and graze on new grass. I know a scientist who even contends that the negro has a stomach like the ruminants. How can you expect him to eat flesh, especially human flesh?"

"Then why kill them?" I objected, for I suddenly felt kind and full of pity. "But I just told you... to civilize them. And it's lots of fun! When, after marching and marching, we arrived in a negro village, they were very frightened! They immediately uttered cries of distress and didn't try to escape—they were so scared—and lay on the ground weeping. We gave them whiskey, for we always kept a large supply of alcohol in our baggage, and when they were drunk we slaughtered them!"

"Bad sportsmanship!" resumed the Norman gentleman with some disgust, for he was doubtless thinking right then of the Tonkin forests, and seeing those marvelous flocks of peacocks flying back and forth.

The night trailed brilliantly on; the sky was ablaze; about us the ocean was spread with great sheets of phosphorescent light. And I was sad, longing for Clara, bored with these gross men, bored with myself and our conversation which offended silence and beauty! Suddenly:

"Do you know Stanley?" Clara asked the explorer.

"Yes, certainly I know him," he replied.

"And what do you think of him?"

"Oh, him!" he said, shaking his head. And as though his mind were a prey to frightful memories, he said, in a grave voice:

"He goes a bit too far, just the same!"

I felt that for some minutes past the captain had wanted to speak. He profited by the moment of respite which followed this declaration:

"I!" he said, "I've done much more than all that. And your little massacres are nothing beside those owing me. I have invented a bullet. *It's* extraordinary. I call it the Dum-Dum, after the name of the little Hindu village where I had the honor to invent it."

"It kills lots of people? More than the others?" Clara asked.

"Oh, dear lady—how can you ask!" he said, laughing. "It's incalculable!" And modestly, however, he added:

"However, that's nothing... it's very small! Imagine a little thing... how do you say?... a little nut, that's it! Imagine a very little nut! It's charming."

"And what a pretty name, captain!" said Clara.

"Very pretty, in fact," agreed the captain, obviously flattered, "very poetic!"

"You'd say—wouldn't you—you'd say it was the name of a fairy in one of Shakespeare's comedies. The fairy Dum-Dum! It enchants me. A laughing, light and quite blond fairy, hopping, dancing and bounding about amid the heather and the sunbeams. And there you are... Dum-Dum!"

"And there you are!" the officer repeated. "absolutely! Besides, it works quite well, adorable lady... I think the most unique thing about it is that, with it, there aren't, so to speak, any more wounded."

"Ah!"

"There are only dead men! That's why it's so really exquisite!" He turned to me, and with an accent of regret in which our mutual patriotism became one, he sighed:

"Ah, if you had had it in France at the time of that frightful Commune! What a triumph!" Then, switching abruptly to another line of thought:

"I sometimes wonder if it's not a tale out of Edgar Allen Poe or a dream of our Thomas de Quincy. But no, since I myself tested that admirable little Dum-Dum. Here is the story. I stood up twelve Hindus—"

"Alive?"

"Naturally! The Emperor of Germany is the one who tries his ballistic experiments on corpses. Confess it's absurd and quite inconclusive. I work with people—not only living, but of robust constitution and in perfect health. At least you can see what you're doing, and where you're going. I am no dreamer. I'm a scientist."

"A thousand pardons, captain! Go right on!"

"Well, I had twelve Hindus stood up, one behind the other, in a geometrically straight line... and fired."

"Well?" Clara interrupted.

"Well, my charming friend, this little Dum-Dum did marvels. Of the twelve Hindus, not one remained standing! The bullet had gone through their twelve bodies which, after the shot, were only twelve heaps of mangled flesh and bones literally ground to dust. Magic—absolute magic! And I'd never dreamed of such an admirable result."

"Admirable indeed, and smacking of the prodigious."

"Doesn't it?" And, thoughtfully, after some seconds of a stirring silence:

"I am looking," he murmured confidentially, "I am looking for something better... something more final. I am looking for a bullet, a little bullet which will annihilate what it hits, leaving nothing... nothing—nothing! Do you understand?"

"How is that? What do you mean, nothing?"

"Oh, very little then!" explained the officer; "scarcely a heap of ashes, or even a light reddish smoke which will immediately vanish. It's possible."

"Automatic incineration, then?"

"Absolutely! Have you considered the innumerable advantages of such an invention? In this way I eliminate army surgeons, nurses, ambulances, military hospitals, pensions for the wounded, etc. It would constitute an incalculable economy, a lightening of governmental budgets, not to mention hygiene! What a conquest for hygiene!"

"And you might call that the Nib—Nibbulled?" I exclaimed.

"Very pretty, very pretty!" applauded the artilleryman who, although he had not at all understood this slangy interruption, started to laugh uproariously, with that honest and frank laugh characteristic of soldiers of all ranks and all nations. When he had calmed down:

"I foresee," he said, "that when France comes to know about this splendid device she will abuse us again in all her newspapers. And it will be the fiercest of your patriots, the very men who shout loudly that not enough millions are ever spent for war, and who only talk of killing and bombardment—it will be those who will once more make England the target for the execration of civilized races. But damn it all! we aren't logical in our state of universal barbarity. What! they admit that shells are explosive, and they don't want bullets to be! Why not? We live under the laws of war. Well, what constitutes war? It consists of massacring as many men as you can in the least possible time. In order to make It more and more murderous and expeditious, you have to find more and more formidable engines of destruction. It makes for humaneness, and also modern progress.

"But captain," I objected, "what about peoples rights? What do you think of that?"

The officer sneered; and lifting his arms to the sky:

"People's rights!" he replied, "it's merely the right we possess to massacre people *en masse* or singly, with shells or bullets—it doesn't matter—provided that people are duly massacred!"

One of the Chinese interposed:

"We are not savages, however!" he said.

"Not savages? and what else are we, I ask you? We are worse savages than the Australian bushmen, since, possessing the knowledge of our savagery, we persist in it. And since it's by war—that is to say theft, pillage and massacre—that we learn to govern, carryon commerce, arbitrate our differences, avenge our honor... Well! We have only to bear with the inconveniences of this state of brutality in which we nevertheless desire to remain. We are brutes—agreed! Let's act like brutes!" Then, in a gentle and profound voice, Clara said:

"Besides, it would be a sacrilege to fight against death. Death is so beautiful!" She arose, white and mysterious beneath the electric deck light. The fine long silk shawl which enveloped her, wrapped her in pale and shifting reflections.

"Till tomorrow!" she said.

All of us stood around her, assiduously attentive. The officer had taken her hand, and kissed it, and I detested his masculine face, his supple loins, his taut limbs and his forceful demeanor. He apologized to his audience:

"Forgive me," he said, "for having allowed myself to be carried away by such a subject, and for having forgotten that in the presence of a woman such as you, one should never talk of anything but love."

Clara replied:

"But captain, when you speak of death, you also speak of love!" She took my arm, and I escorted her to her cabin where her women were waiting to prepare her for bed.

The entire evening I was haunted by massacre and destruction. My sleep was quite feverish that night. Capering about over the red heather and amid the rays of a bloody sun, I saw the blond, laughing and leaping little fairy, Dum-Dum... the little fairy, Dum-Dum, which had the eyes, the mouth and all the unknown and unveiled flesh of Clara.

PART 7

One time my friend and I were leaning side by side against the rail, and looking at the sea and the sky. The day would soon be done. In the sky, great birds—blue kingfishers—were following the ship, balancing themselves with the exquisite movements of a ballerina; on the sea, schools of flying-fish rose at our approach and, gleaming in the sun, dove in farther off to reappear immediately, scudding over the water which was blue as brilliant turquoise that day. Then schools of jellyfish, red jellyfish, green jellyfish, purple, rose and mauve, floated like heaps of flowers on the soft surface, and their colors were so magnificent that every moment Clara uttered cries of admiration as she pointed them out to me. Then, suddenly, she asked:

"Tell me. What is the name of these marvelous creatures?"

I might have improvised bizarre names or sought scientific nomenclature. I did not even attempt it. Moved by an immediate, spontaneous and violent need of frankness:

"I don't know!" I firmly replied.

I felt I was lost, that I was also losing this vague and charming dream which had cradled my hopes and soothed my anxieties—irrevocably losing it; that I was going to fall back even deeper than ever into the inevitable mire of my life as a pariah. I felt all this. But there was something stronger than all that in me, which commanded me to wash myself of all my impostures, all my lies; all this veritable abuse of confidence, by which I had fraudulently achieved, in a cowardly and criminal fashion, the friendship of a person who had had faith in my words.

"No, really, I don't know!" I repeated, giving to this simple negation a quality of dramatic exaltation of which it did not admit.

"How strangely you say that! Are you crazy? What's the matter with you?" said Clara, astonished at the sound of my voice and the strange incoherence of my gestures.

"I don't know... I don't know... I don't know!" And to add more force of conviction to that triple 'I don't know!' I violently struck the rail three times.

"What, you don't know? A scientist... a naturalist?"

"I am not a scientist, Miss Clara, I am not a naturalist—I am nothing," I cried. "A wretch, yes... I am a wretch! I've lied to you, shamefully lied. You must know the sort of man I am. Listen to me..."

Panting, agitated, I related my life: Eugene Mortain, Mme. G——, the imposture of my mission, all my filth, all my mire. I took an atrocious delight in accusing myself, making myself viler, more of an outcast and still blacker than I was. When I had finished this distressing tale, I said to my friend, in a flood of tears:

"Now it's all over! You will detest me, despise me, like the others, you will turn away from me with disgust. And you will be right, and I won't complain. It's frightful! But I can't live like this any longer. I want no more lies between us." I wept copiously, and I stuttered incoherent words, like a child.

"It's horrible! It's horrible! and I who... for after all... it's true, I swear to you! I who... you understand. A whirlpool, that's it... a whirlpool. I was caught in a whirlpool. I didn't know it. And then your soul... ah, your soul!... your gentle soul... your pure glances... and your... your dear... yes, after all... you know it well... your dear welcome, it was my salvation... my redemption... my... my. It's horrible... it's horrible! I'm losing all that! It's horrible!"

While I was talking and weeping Miss Clara looked at me attentively. Oh, that look! Never—no never, shall I forget the glance that adorable woman fixed upon me—an extraordinary glance, which held at the same time astonishment, joy, pity, and love—yes, love—and malice too, and irony... and everything. A glance which entered into me, penetrated me, probed me and overwhelmed my soul and my flesh.

"Well," she said simply, "that doesn't astonish me very much. And I honestly believe all scientists are like you."

Without taking her eyes off me, she gave her clear and pretty laugh—a laugh like the song of a bird:

"I knew one of them," she went on. "He was a naturalist... of your type. He had been sent by the British government to study the coffee-parasite on the plantations in Ceylon. Well, for three months, he did not leave Colombo. He spent his time playing poker and getting drunk on champagne."

Still looking at me with a strange, profound and voluptuous look—always focused on me—after some seconds of silence she added, in a tone of commiseration in which it seemed to me I heard all the exultation of forgiveness:

"Oh the little swine!"

I no longer knew what to say, or whether to laugh or weep again, or whether to kneel at her feet. Timidly, I mumbled:

"Then... you're not angry with me? You don't despise me? You forgive me?"

"Silly!" she said. "Oh, the little fool!" "Clara! Clara! Is it possible?" I cried, almost fainting for joy. As the dinner-bell had long since rung and there was no longer anyone on that part of the deck, I came closer to Clara, so close that I could feel her loins trembling against me, and her heart beating. And seizing her hands, which she left in mine, while my heart rose tempestuously in me, I cried:

"Clara! Clara! do you love me? Ah, I beg you! Do you love me?" She replied feebly:

"I'll tell you that, this evening... in my cabin!"

In her eyes I saw the flicker of a green flame, a terrible flame which terrified me. She withdrew her hands from my grasp, a heavy line suddenly crossed her forehead, and with her head bowed, she was silent and looked at the sea.

What was she thinking about? I could tell nothing. And, looking out to sea myself, I thought:

While I was an honorable man in her eyes, she did not love me. But the minute she understood what I was, when she breathed the true and foul odor of my soul, love was born in her—for she *does* love me! Well, well! There is nothing real, then, except evil!

Evening had come; then, without any twilight, it was night. An ineffable sweetness floated in the air. The ship sailed through boiling phosphorescent foam. Great lights skimmed over the sea. You'd have thought the fairies were rising from the sea, trailing long fiery mantles on the surface, and shaking and hurling great handfuls of golden pearls into the water.

PART 8

One morning, coming out on deck, I could make out, thanks to the transparence of the atmosphere, and as clearly as though I were treading its soil, the enchanted island of Ceylon; that green and red island crowned by the fairylike rosy whiteness of Adam's Peak. We had already been warned of its approach the evening before by the new perfumes of the sea and a mysterious invasion of butterflies which, after accompanying the ship for a few hours, suddenly disappeared. And without desiring anything more, both Clara and I found it exquisite that the island had extended us a welcome through the medium of these dazzling and poetic messengers. I had then reached such a point of sentimental poeticism that the mere sight of a butterfly made all the strings of tenderness and ecstasy vibrate in my breast.

But that morning the actual sight of Ceylon caused me great anguish—and more than anguish—terror. What I caught a glimpse of over there beyond the waves, which were then the color of forget-me-not, was not a territory, not a port, nor the burning curiosity of everything that stirs the ultimately lifted veil of the unknown in man. It was the brutal summons to evil life, the return to my forsaken instincts, the bitter and desolating reawakening of all which, during the crossing, had slumbered in me, and which I had thought dead! It was something more distressing, of which I had never dreamed, and which it was impossible for me not only to understand, but even conceive of its possible reality: the end of the prodigious dream which Clara's love had been for me. For the first time, a woman held me. I was her slave; I desired none but her; I wanted none but her. Nothing any longer existed outside or beyond her. Instead of extinguishing the fire of my love, every day possession fanned its flame. I descended further into the burning gulf of her desire each time, and every day I realized more strongly that my entire life would be exhausted seeking to reach its bottom! How could I accept the fact that, after having been conquered—soul, body and brain—by this irrevocable, indissoluble and martyrizing love, I would have to immediately give it up? Madness! This love was a part of me, like my own flesh; it had taken the place of my blood and marrow; it possessed me entirely; it was I! To separate me from it meant to separate me from myself; it meant to kill me. Worse still! It meant the extravagant nightmare that my head was in Ceylon, my feet in China, separated by abysses of ocean, and that I would continue to live in these two stumps which could never be reunited! That the very next day I would no longer possess those swooning eyes, those devouring lips, the nightly renewed miracle of that body with its divine contours and savage embraces; and, after long spasms as powerful as sin and as deep as death, that naive stammering, those little laughs, those little tears, those languid little songs of a child or a bird—was it possible! And I would lose all that was more necessary for breathing than my lungs; more necessary for thinking than my brain; more necessary for nourishing my veins with warm blood than my heart! Impossible! I belonged to Clara like the coal belongs to the fire which devours and consumes it. Both to her and me, a separation had seemed so inconceivable and so insanely fantastic, so totally contrary to the laws of nature and life, that we had never spoken of it. The evening before, our communing hearts had thought of nothing—and without even mentioning it—but the eternity of the voyage, as though the ship which bore us on might carry us thus forever, and never, never arrive anywhere. For to arrive somewhere means to die!

Yet, here I was about to get off, plunge into that green and that red, disappear over there in that unknown... more frightfully alone than ever! And here was Clara, soon to be no more than a phantom, then a little grey speck scarcely visible in space... then nothing... nothing... nothing! Ah, anything rather than that! Ah, let the sea engulf us both.

The sea was gentle, calm and radiant. It exhaled the perfumes of a Utopian shore, a blossoming orchard and a bed of love, which made me weep. The deck was thronged; nothing but happy faces, eyes strained by waiting and curiosity:

"We're entering the bay... we're in the bay!"

"I see the shore."

"I see the trees."

"I see the lighthouse."

"We're here... we're here!"

Each of these exclamations fell heavily on my heart. I no longer wanted before me the sight of this island, still distant but so implacably clear—which every turn of the screw brought nearer to me, and turning from it, I gazed at the infinity of the sky into which I prayed I might disappear, like those birds over there, so high, which flew for a moment through the air and disappeared so easily.

Clara hastened to join me. Was it from having loved too much? Was it from having wept too long? For her eyelids were darkened, and her eyes with their dark blue rings expressed more than sadness: there was actually an ardent pity in them, both belligerent and commiserative. Beneath her heavy golden-brown hair, her forehead was crossed by a line of shadow; that line which was there in desire, as well as in pain. A strangely intoxicating perfume emanated from her hair. She said to me, simply, this single word:

"Already?"

"Alas!" I sighed.

She finished adjusting her hat, a little sailor-hat which she fastened with a long gold pin. Her raised arms made her breasts stand out, and I could see their sculptural curves outlined beneath the white blouse which enveloped them. She continued in a voice which trembled slightly:

"Had you thought about it?"

"No!"

Clara bit her lips.

"And then?" she said.

I did not answer. I had not the strength to answer. My head empty, my heart torn, I should have liked to slip into oblivion. She was moved, very pale, except her mouth which seemed redder, and heavy with kisses. For a long time her eyes questioned me with great intensity.

"The ship touches at Colombo two days. Then it leaves again. Did you know it?

"Yes! yes!"

"And then?"

"And then... it's over!"

"Can I do something for you?"

"Nothing... thanks! for it's all over!"

And stifling my sobs in my throat, I stuttered:

"You've been everything to me. You've been more than everything to me! Don't speak to me any more, I beg you! It's too distressing... too uselessly distressing. Don't speak to me any more... for now, everything is over!"

"Nothing is ever over," proclaimed Clara; "nothing, not even death!"

A bell rang. Ah, that bell! How it tolled in my heart! How it tolled the death-knell of my heart!

The passengers crowded on the deck, shouting, exclaiming, questioning each other, leveling lorgnettes opera-glasses and cameras at the approaching island. The Norman gentleman, pointing out the masses of foliage, was describing the jungles impenetrable to the hunter. And amid the tumult and jostling, indifferent and reflective, their hands crossed in their wide sleeves, the two Chinese continued their slow, grave, daily promenade, like two priests reciting their breviaries.

"We're here!"

"Hurrah! hurrah! We're here!" "I see the city.'"

"Is that the city?'"

"No! that's a coral ledge..."

"I can make out the wharf..."

"No! No!"

"What's that coming, out there on the sea?"

Already, in the distance, a little flotilla of barks with their pink sails was coming out to the steamer. The two smokestacks, belching clouds of black smoke, covered the sea with a mourning-pall, and the siren moaned forever... forever. No one paid any attention to us. Clara asked me, in a tone of imperious tenderness:

"Well! what's to become of you?"

"I don't know! And what difference does it make?

I was lost... I met you. You have held me from the brink of the abyss for a few days. Now I'll fall back into it. It was inevitable!"

"Why inevitable? You're a child! And you have no confidence in me. Do you really think it was by chance you met me?" After a long silence, she added:

"It's so simple! I have powerful friends in China. They could undoubtedly do a lot for you! Would you like—"

I did not give her time to finish:

"No, not that!" I begged, resisting feebly. "Anyway—above all, not that! I understand you... Don't say any more."

"You're a child," Clara repeated, "and talk like they do in Europe, darling. And you have stupid scruples, like in Europe. In China life is free, joyous, complete, unconventional, unprejudiced, lawless... at least for us. No other limits to liberty than yourself... or to love, than the triumphant variety of your desire. Europe and its hypocritical, barbaric civilization is a lie. What else do you do there except lie—lie to yourself and others, lie about everything you recognize in your heart to be true? You're obliged to pretend respect for people and institutions you think absurd. You live attached in a cowardly fashion to moral and social conventions you despise, condemn, and know lack all foundation. It is that permanent contradiction between your ideas and desires and all the dead formalities and vain pretenses of your civilization which makes you sad, troubled and unbalanced. In that intolerable conflict you lose all joy of life and all feeling of personality, because at every moment they suppress and restrain and check the free play of your powers. That's the poisoned and mortal wound of the civilized world. With us, there's nothing like it... you'll see! In Canton I own a palace amid marvelous gardens, where everything is conducive to a free life, and to love. What are you afraid of? What are you leaving behind? Who cares about you! When you don't love me any more, or when you are too unhappy... you go away."

"Clara! Clara!" I implored.

She stamped sharply on the deck of the ship:

"You don't know me yet," she said, "you don't know what I am, and you want to leave me already! Do I frighten you? Are you a coward?"

"I could not live without you! Without you, I could only die!"

"Well, stop trembling... and stop weeping... and come with me!" A light flashed in her green pupils, and in a low, almost raucous voice, she said:

"I'll teach you terrible things... divine things... you'll know at last what love real-

ly is! I promise you'll descend with me to the very depths of the mystery of love...
and death!" And smiling an evil smile which made a shiver run through my bones,
she said again:

"Poor baby! You thought yourself a great debauchee... a great rebel! Ah! your
little remorse... do you remember! And now your soul is as timid as a little
child's!"

It was true! I had vainly boasted of being an uncompromising swine, thought
myself superior to moral prejudices. I still occasionally heard the voice of duty
and honor which, at certain moments of nervous depression, rose from the troubled depths of my conscience. Whose honor? what duty? What a sink of madness
is man's mind! In what way would my honor—my honor!—be compromised, in
what way would I shirk my duty if I continued my voyage all the way to China,
instead of rotting away in Ceylon? Had I actually crawled far enough into the skin
of a scientist to imagine that I was going to 'study the pelagic ooze,' or discover
'the cell,' by plunging into the gulfs of the Singhalese coast? This quite grotesque
idea, that I had taken my embryological mission seriously, quickly led me back to
the reality of my situation. What! fate or a miracle had willed it that I meet a
woman, divinely beautiful, rich, exceptional, and whom I loved and who loved
me, and who offered me an extraordinary life, joy in abundance, unique sensations, libertine adventures, luxurious protection... salvation after all... and more
than salvation—bliss! And I was going to let it all slip through my fingers! Once
more the demon of perversity, that stupid demon to whom I owed all my unhappi-
ness—because I had so stupidly obeyed him—intervened again and advised me
hypocritically to resist an un-hoped-for adventure, a fairy-tale come to life, which
would never be encountered again and which I ardently desired from the bottom
of my heart, and which had actually materialized. No... no! It was too stupid, after
all!

"You're right," I said to Clara, ascribing solely to my defeat in love a submission which also included all my instincts of laziness and debauchery; you're right;
I wouldn't be worthy of your eyes, your mouth and your heart... of all that paradise and that hell which is YOU, if I hesitated any longer. And then, I could not...
I could not lose you. I can conceive of everything but that. You are right, I belong
to you; lead me where you wish. To suffer... to die... it makes no difference! since
you—whom I still do not know—are my fate!"

"Oh, baby! baby! baby!" said Clara in a singular tone whose true expression I
could not unravel—whether it was joy, irony or pity! Then, almost maternally, she
admonished me:

"Now, don't worry about anything. Try to be happy. Stay here... look at the marvelous island. I'm going to arrange with the commissioner for your new status on
board."

"Clara."

"Don't be afraid. I know what to say." And as I was about to object:

"Shush! Aren't you my baby, darling? You must obey. And then, you don't know... " And she disappeared into the crowd of passengers huddled on deck, many of whom were already carrying their yalises and their lighter baggage.

It had been decided that Clara and I would spend the two days in port at Colombo visiting the city and the suburbs, where my friend had stayed and which she knew thoroughly. The heat there was torrid, so torrid that the coolest places—by comparison—in this atrocious land (where the scientists have located the earthly paradise), such as the gardens on the banks of the strand, seemed to me to be stifling steam rooms. The majority of our traveling-companions did not dare to risk this fiery temperature, which stripped them of the slightest desire to go out and the vaguest desire to move. I can still see them, ridiculous and moaning in the lobby of the hotel, wrapped in moistened and steaming napkins—elegant apparel renewed every quarter of an hour—which transformed the noblest part of their person into a chimney-pipe, crowned with its plume of steam. Slumped into rocking-chairs under the *punka,* their brains atrophied, their lungs congested, they drank iced drinks prepared for them by the boys who, by the color of their skin and the structure of their bodies, recalled the naive gingerbread men of our Parisian fairs; while other boys of the same hue and the same build kept the mosquitoes away from them by great sweeps of a fan. As for me, I recovered—perhaps a bit too soon—all my gaiety and all my sprightly wit. My scruples had vanished; I no longer felt in a poetical mood. Relieved of my anxiety about the future, I once more became the man I was when I left Marseille; the stupid and critical Parisian, 'who can't be fooled'; the boulevardier who won't listen to nonsense, and who knows all about nature... even the tropics!

To me Colombo seemed a boring and ridiculous city, unpicturesque and lacking in mystery. It was half Protestant, half Buddhist, besotted as a bronze and sullen as a pastor, and with what joy I congratulated myself on having miraculously escaped the profound boredom of its streets, its dead sky and its coarse vegetation. And I made jokes about the cocoanut trees, which I did not fail to compare to frightful plucked feather-dusters, as well as about the great plants which I accused of having been cut out of painted sheet-iron and polished zinc, by malicious workmen. Walking on Slave Island, which is the *Bois* of the place, or in Pettah, which is its *Mouffetard* quarter, we only encountered horrible Englishwomen out of an operetta, togged out as though for a carnival, in light costumes, half-European and half Hindu; and Singhalese still more horrible than the Englishwomen, old at twelve years, wrinkled as prunes, twisted as aged vine-stalks, caved in like ruined straw huts, with gums like bleeding wounds, lips burned by the areca-nut and teeth the color of an old pipe. I sought in vain for the voluptuous women, the negresses with their wise love-techniques, the pert little lace makers of whom that liar Eugene Mortain had spoken, with their eyes so significantly provocative. And with all my heart I pitied the poor scientists they sent here, with their problematic mission of discovering the secret of life.

But I realized Clara had no taste for these facile and Coarse jokes, and I found it prudent to attenuate them, not wishing to wound her either in her fervent cult or nature, or shrink in her estimation. On several occasions I had noticed that she listened to me with painful astonishment.

"Why are you so gay?" She said to me, "I don't like people to be gay like that, darling. It hurts me. When you're gay it's because you're not in love. Love is serious, sad and profound." Which, however, did not prevent her from bursting into laughter apropos of anything or nothing. In this way she encouraged me greatly in a deception which I concocted, and which was this:

Among the letters of recommendation I had brought from Paris, there was one to a certain Sir Oscar Terwick who, aside from his other scientific titles, was the president of the *Association of Tropical Embryology and British Entomology* at Colombo. At the hotel where I sought information, I learned, in fact, that Sir Oscar Terwick was quite a personage, the author of renowned works, and, in a word, a very great scientist. I decided to go to see him. Such a visit could no longer be dangerous to me, and besides, I was not sorry to know and make contact with an actual embryologist. He lived far off in a suburb called Kolpetty, which was, so to speak, the *Passy* of Colombo. There, in the midst of luxurious gardens, graced by the inevitable cocoanut tree, in spacious and bizarre villas, the rich merchants and notable officials of the city lived. Clara desired to accompany me. She waited for me in the carriage not far from the savant's house, in a sort of little square shaded by immense teakwood trees.

Sir Oscar Terwick received me politely—nothing more. He was a very tall man, very slender, very dry, very red in the face, and his white beard fell to his navel and was cut squarely like a pony's tail. He wore great trousers of yellow silk, and his hairy torso was wrapped in a sort of shawl of light wool. He gravely read the letter I handed him and, after having examined me out of the corner of his eye with a suspicious air—was he suspicious of me or of himself?—he asked me:

"You... are... embryologist?"

I nodded my head in assent.

"All right!" he clucked. And making the gesture of trailing a net in the sea, he went on:

"You... are... embryologist? *Yes... You...* You... *comme ca... dans le mer...* fish... fish... little fish?"

"Little fish... absolutely... little fish," I insisted, repeating the imitative gesture of the scientist.

"Dans le mer?"

"Yes!... yes."

Tres interessant!... tres joli... tres curious! Yes."

Jabbering like this—and both of us continuing to drag our fanciful nets 'in the sea'—the noted scientist led me to a bamboo console on which three plaster busts were standing, crowned with artificial lotus. Indicating them respectively with his thumb, he presented them to me in so comically serious a tone I almost burst out laughing.

"Master Darwin—very great—naturalist... very, very... great!... *Yes!*"

I made a deep bow.

"Master Haeckel... *ires grand naturaliste...* Not as great as he, no!... *Mais tres grand!* Master Haeckel *ici... comme ca... lui... dans Ie mer...* little fish."

I bowed again. And he exclaimed in a louder voice, laying his whole hand, red as a crab, upon the third bust:

"Master Coqueline! Tres grand naturaliste... du miouseum... comment appelez?... du miouseum. Grevin—Yes!—Grevin! Tres joli—tres curious!" "Very interesting!" I agreed.

"Yes!"

After which he dismissed me.

I gave Clara a detailed and acted version of this interview. She laughed like a mad woman.

"Oh baby!... baby... baby... how funny you are, you little devil!"

This was the sole scientific episode of my mission. And I appreciated then what embryology was!

The next morning, after a savage night of love, we put to sea again en route to China.

THE GARDEN
PART 1

"Why haven't you spoken to me yet about our dear Annie? Haven't you told her about my arrival? Won't she come today? Is she still as beautiful as ever?"

What! Don't you know, darling? Annie is dead." "Dead!" I exclaimed. "It's not possible. You're teasing me."

I looked at Clara. Divinely calm and pretty, naked in a transparent tunic of yellow silk, she was languidly stretched out on a tiger skin. Her head lay among the cushions, and with her hands, loaded with rings, she played with a long wisp of her flowing hair. A Laos dog with red hair slept beside her, its muzzle resting on her thigh and a paw upon her breast.

"What?" Clara went on, "didn't you know? Why, that's funny!" All smiles, and stretching like a supple animal, she explained to me:

"It was horrible, my dear! Annie died... died of that frightful scourge called elephantiasis... for everything here is frightful... love... disease... and the flowers! Never have I wept so much, I assure you. I loved her so much—so much! And she was so beautiful!"

She added, with a long and charming sigh:

"Never again will we know the bitter taste of her kisses! It's a great misfortune!"

"Then it's really true!" I stammered. "But how did it happen?"

"I don't know. There are so many mysteries here, so many things that can't be understood. Both of us often used to go out on the river in the evening. I must tell you that there was a bayadere from Benares, in a flower—boat... a bewitching creature, my dear, whom the priests had taught certain cursed rites of the ancient Brahman cults. Perhaps it was that... or something else. One night when we were returning from the river, Annie complained of violent pains in the head and loins, and the next day her body was all covered with little purple spots. Her skin, rosier and finer than the althea flower, was hardening—thickening, swelling, and became an ashy grey. Great tumors and monstrous tubercles arose. It was something frightful. And the disease which at first had attacked her legs, reached her thighs, her abdomen, her breasts, her face. Oh, her face, her face! Imagine an enormous pouch, a disgusting sack, all grey and striated with brown blood, and which hung and swayed with the least movement she made. Her eyes—her eyes, my darling! You could see no more of them than tiny, reddish, oozing holes. I still wonder if it's possible!"

She twined the golden lock of her hair about her fingers. In his sleep the dog's paw had slipped along her silk tunic, entirely uncovering the globe of her breast, whose nipple arose, pink as a young flower.

"Yes, I still wonder sometimes whether I'm not dreaming," she said.

"Clara... Clara!" I implored, aghast with horror, "don't tell me any more. I'd like the image of our divine Annie to remain intact in my memory. What can I do now to dispel this nightmare? Ah, Clara! don't say any more; or talk to me about Annie when she was so beautiful... when she was too beautiful!"

Clara did not listen to me, but continued:

"Annie isolated herself... shut herself up in her house, alone with a Chinese housekeeper who took care of her. She had sent all her women away, and no longer wanted to see anyone... not even me. She summoned the cleverest practitioners of England. In vain, you may be Sure. The most celebrated sorcerers of Tibet—those who know the magic words and resuscitate the dead declared themselves powerless. You never recover from that disease; but you never die of it. It's frightful! "Then she killed herself. A few drops of poison, and that was the end of the most beautiful of women."

Terror sealed my lips. I looked at Clara, unable to utter a single word.

"I learned from that Chinese woman," Clara continued, "a really curious detail, which fascinated me. You know how much Annie loved pearls. She owned some incomparable specimens... the most marvelous, I believe, that ever existed. You also remember the almost physical joy, the carnal ecstasy, with which she adorned herself with them. Well, when she was sick that passion became a mania with her... a fury, like love! All day long she loved to touch them, caress them and kiss them j she made cushions of them, necklaces, capes, cloaks. Then this extraordinary thing happened; the pearls died on her skin: first they tarnished, little by little... little by little they grew dim, and no light was reflected in their luster any more and, in a few days, tainted by the disease, they changed into tiny balls of ash. They were dead, dead like people, my darling. Did you know that pearls had souls? I think it's fascinating and delicious. And since then, I think of it every day." After a short silence, she went on:

"And that's not all! Annie often expressed the desire to be carried to the little Parsee cemetery when she died—over there, on the hill of the Blue Dog. She wanted her body to be torn to pieces by the beaks of vultures. You know what strange and violent ideas she had on all subjects? Well, the vultures refused this royal feast she offered them. They flew away from her corpse, uttering frightful cries. We had to cremate her. It was awful!"

"But why didn't you write me all that?" I reproached Clara.

With slow and charming gestures, Clara smoothed the red—gold of her hair and caressed the red fur of the dog, which had awakened, and she said carelessly:

"Really? Didn't I write you anything about that? Are you sure? Doubtless I'd forgotten. Poor Annie!"

Again she spoke:

Since that great misfortune, everything here bores me. I am too lonely. I would like to die... to die... I too. Ah, I assure you! And if you hadn't come back, I honestly believe I would be dead already."

She laid her head back on the cushions, bared her breast still more, and with a smile... the strange smile of both a child and a harlot:

"Do my breasts still please you? Do you still think me beautiful? Then why were you gone so... so long? Yes... yes... I know... don't say anything more, don't answer... I know. You are a little fool, my darling!"

I would have greatly liked to weep; but I couldn't. I would have greatly liked to speak again, but again I was unable.

And we were in the garden, under the gilded kiosk, where the glycines hung in clusters, white clusters; and We finished having tea. Sparkling scarabees swarmed among the leaves, cetonia beetles buzzed and died in the swooning hearts of the roses, and through the open door on the northern side, rising from the pool around which in the soft, mauve shadows, storks were sleeping, we could see the long stems of yellow irises, streaked with purple. Suddenly Clara asked me:

"Would you like us to go and feed the Chinese Convicts? It's very curious... very amusing. It's really the only original and fashionable diversion we have here, in this God-forsaken corner of China. Would you like to, darling?"

I felt fatigue, my head was heavy, all my being racked by the fever of that frightful climate. Besides, the story of Annie's death had overwhelmed my spirit. And the heat, moreover, was deadly as poison.

"I don't know what you asked me, Clara dear, but I haven't recovered from that long trip across plains and plains... forests and forests. And that sun! I fear it more than death! Besides, I wanted so much to be alone with you, and you with me... today."

"That's right! If we were in Europe, and I'd asked you to accompany me to the races or the theatre, you wouldn't have hesitated. But it's so much nicer than the races."

"Be kind! Tomorrow, if you like?"

"Oh, tomorrow!" replied Clara, with an expression of surprise and her air of gentle reproach. "Always tomorrow! Don't you know that it's impossible tomorrow? Tomorrow—why it's strictly forbidden. The doors of the bagnio are closed, even to me. You can only feed the convicts on Wednesday; how is it you didn't know? If we miss this visit today, we'll have to wait a whole long week. How boring it would be! A whole week, think of it! Come, darling booby. Oh, come! I beg you. You could at least do that much for me.

She lifted herself up on the cushions. The gaping tunic revealed patches of her ardent rosy flesh below the waist, amid the clouds of the silk. From a gold bonbon dish on a lacquer platter she took a quinine pellet with the tips of her fingers, and commanding me to approach, she put it gently between my lips.

"You'll see how exciting it is... so exciting! You have no idea, darling. And how much more I'll love you tonight. How madly I'll love you tonight! Swallow, darling... swallow!"

Somber lights gleamed in her eyes, and as I was still sad and hesitant, to overcome my last objections, she said:

"Listen! I've seen robbers hung in England; I've seen bullfights, and anarchists garroted in Spain. In Russia I've seen beautiful young girls whipped to death by soldiers. In Italy I've seen living phantoms—spectres of famine—disinter the bodies of cholera victims and eat them eagerly. I've seen thousands of souls beside a stream in India, stark naked, writhing and dying of the plague. In Berlin one evening I saw a woman I had loved the night before—a splendid creature in pink tights—I saw her devoured by a lion in a cage. All the horrors, all the human tortures—I have seen them. It was very lovely! But I've seen nothing lovelier... you understand?... than the Chinese convicts. It's lovelier than everything! You can't possibly know. I tell you, you can't possibly know. Annie and I never missed a Wednesday. Come, I beg you!"

"Since it's so lovely, my dear Clara, and it gives you so much pleasure," I answered sadly, "let's go and feed the convicts."

"Really, you want to?"

Clara expressed her delight, clapping her hands like a baby whose governess has just given it permission to torture a little dog. Then she jumped up on my knees, affectionate and feline, and threw her bare arms around my neck... and her hair smothered me, blinded my face with golden flames and intoxicating perfumes.

"How nice you are... dear... dear darling. Kiss my lips... kiss my neck... kiss my hair... dear little devil!"

Her hair possessed so powerful an animal odor and was so electrically stimulating, that its mere contact with my skin instantaneously made me forget fever, fatigue and pain... and I immediately felt heroic ardor and new strength flowing and surging through my veins.

"Oh, what fun we'll have, sweetheart. When I go to see the convicts, it makes me dizzy, and thrills run through my entire body, like thrills of passion. It seems to me, you see... it seems to me that I'm sinking to the depths of my being... to the very deepest recesses of my being. Your mouth... give me your mouth... your mouth... your mouth!" Then nimbly, quickly joyful and shameless, followed by the bounding red dog, she went to the women who dressed her.

I was no longer very sad; I was no longer very tired. Clara's kiss, the taste of which I still had on my lips like a magic drop of opium—dulled my pain, relieved the throbbing of my fever, almost completely dispelled the monstrous image of Annie's death. And I looked calmly at the garden.

Calmly?

The garden descended in gentle slopes, graced everywhere by rare herbs and precious plants. An alley of enormous camphor trees began at the kiosk where I sat, and ended at a red door in the form of a temple, which opened out on the countryside. Between the leafy branches of the gigantic trees which concealed the view on the left, I could see the stream which gleamed like polished silver in the sun. I tried to become interested in the multiple decorations of the garden, in its strange flowers and grotesque vegetation. A man with two indolent panthers in leash, crossed the path. Here, in the center of a lawn, there stood an immense bronze representing some divinity or other—obscene and cruel. There, cranes with blue plumage and red-throated toucans from tropical America, sacred pheasants, golden—crowned and golden-breasted ducks clad in brilliant purple like ancient warriors, and multicolored wading-birds, sought the shade beside the clumps of foliage. But neither the birds nor the felines, nor the gods, nor the flowers could hold my attention, nor the bizarre palace on my right which, between the dwarf cedars and the bamboos, lifted its bright terraces covered with flowers, and its shady balconies and covered roofs. My thoughts were elsewhere... very, very far away across the seas and the forests. They were centered in me, plunged into myself... in the very depths of my being! Calmly?

Scarcely had Clara disappeared behind the foliage of the garden than I was seized with remorse at being there. Why had I returned? What madness and what cowardice had I obeyed? She had said to me one day you remember—on the ship: 'When you are too unhappy, you will go away.' I had believed myself fortified by my infamous past and, in fact, I was only a worried and feeble child. Unhappy? Ah yes, I had been that—unhappy to the point of the worst possible torture; to the point of a prodigious disgust with myself. And I had gone away! With really vindictive irony I had profited by an English mission passing through Canton to escape from Clara—I was decidedly destined to follow missions. I was going to explore the lesser known regions of Annam. It meant forgetfulness, perhaps... and perhaps death. For two years—two long, cruel years, I had tramped and tramped—and there was neither forgetfulness nor death. Despite fatigue, danger and the accursed fever—I was not able for a day, nor for a minute, to cure myself of the frightful poison that woman had injected into my flesh—that woman to whom I felt myself attached and riveted. And I realized that the very thing that held me to her was the frightful rottenness of her soul and her crimes of love. She was a monster, and I loved her for being a monster! I had believed—had I really?—that her love could uplift me... and here I had descended even lower, to the floor of the tainted gulf out of which, having once inhaled its odor, you never climb again.

Often, in the depths of the forests, haunted by fever after the halts—in my tent—I tried to kill her monstrous and persistent image with opium. And the opium evoked her for me in a more material fashion, and more living, more imperious than ever. Then I wrote her mad, insulting and scurrilous letters—letters in which the most violent loathing was mingled with the most abject adoration. She answered me with charming, naive and plaintive letters which I sometimes found in the cities and post-offices we passed. She confessed to be unhappy over my abandonment... wept, supplicated and called me back. She found no other excuse than this: 'You must understand, my dear—' she wrote, 'that I have no soul for your horrid Europe. I bear in me the soul of old China, which is much more beautiful. Isn't it desolating that you can't grasp that idea?' In this way I learned that she had left Canton, where she could no longer live without me, to go and live with Annie in a city farther south in China, 'which is marvelous'. Ah, how could

I have so long resisted the desire to abandon my companions and hasten to that sublime and cursed city, that exquisite and agonizing hell where Clara breathed and lived, in the midst of fierce and unknown lusts for lack of which I was then dying. And I came back to her, like an assassin returns to the very scene of his crime...

Laughter in the foliage, little cries, the bounding of a dog. It was Clara. She was dressed, half as a Chinese, half as a European. A blouse of pale mauve silk, embroidered with faintly gilded flowers, wrapped her in a thousand folds, outlining her lithe body and her rich contours. She had on a great hat of pale straw, in whose depths her face appeared like a pink flower in a slight shadow. And her little feet were clad in yellow leather. When she entered the kiosk, it was like an explosion of perfumes.

"This is a queer get-up, isn't it? Oh, the sad, sad man from Europe, who hasn't laughed once since he returned! Don't you think me beautiful?"

As I didn't get up from the divan on which I was stretched:

"Quick! quick! darling—for we have to make the grand tour. I'll put on my gloves on the way. Come... come along! No, no... not you!" she added, gently, repulsing the dog which was yelping, leaping and wagging its tail. She called a boy and instructed him to follow us with the provision-basket and the little pitchfork.

"Ah," she explained to me, "it's very amusing! A darling little basket woven by the best basket-maker in China; and the pitchfork... you'll see—a darling little fork whose teeth are platinum inlaid with gold, and the handle is made of green jade... green as the sky at the first flush of dawn... green as poor Annie's eyes! Come now—don't make that awful funereal face, darling... and come quickly... quickly!"

And we started to walk in the sun, that horrible sun which blackened the grass, withered the peonies in the garden and bore down on my skull like a heavy laden helmet.

PART 2

The Bagnio is on the other side of the river, whose black and pestilential waters slowly and sinisterly flow between their low banks outside the city limits. To get to it, you have to make a long detour, and cross a bridge on which the Convict Meat Market is held every Wednesday, in the midst of a fashionable throng.

Clara had refused to take a palanquin. We went down through the garden situated outside the city walls, on foot, and by a path bordered here and there by brown stones, thick hedges of white roses or clipped privet hedges, we reached the suburbs at the point where the dwindling city almost becomes countryside; where the houses, now shacks, are at great intervals from each other, and are situated in little yards fenced about with bamboo. From there on, there are only blossoming orchards, truck-gardens or empty lots. Men stripped to the waist and wearing bell-shaped hats worked laboriously in the sun planting lilies—those beautiful tiger lilies whose petals resemble the legs of marine spiders and whose tasty bulbs serve as nourishment for the rich. We passed some wretched sheds where potters were turning their pots, where rag pickers squatting before huge baskets were taking stock of the morning harvest, while a flock of hungry and cackling condors wheeled back and forth above them. Not far off under an enormous fig tree, we saw a gentle and meticulous old man who was bathing birds at the edge of a fountain. Every few minutes we crossed in front of palanquins carrying foreign sailors, already drunk, towards the city. And behind us, sweltering and huddled, sprawling over the high hill, the city with its temples and strange red, green, and yellow houses, lay shimmering in the dazzling light.

Clara walked rapidly, unmoved by my fatigue. Heedless of the sun which charged the atmosphere and burned our skin despite our parasols, she walked freely—supple, bold and happy. Occasionally, in a tone of merry reproach, she said to me:

"How slow you are, sweetheart. *God*, you're slow! You're not getting anywhere. If only the doors of the bagnio aren't open when we get there, and the convicts aren't already gorged! It would be frightful! Oh, how I would detest you!"

From time to time she gave me a hamamelis tablet, whose property is to stimulate the respiration; and, her eyes mocking me:

"Oh, little woman!... little woman... little, insignificant woman!" Then, half laughing, half angry, she started to run, and I had great difficulty in following her. Several times I had to stop and catch my breath. I felt that my arteries would burst in my chest. And Clara repeated, in her warbling voice:

"Little woman! Little, insignificant woman."

The path comes out upon the quay of the stream. Two great steamers were unloading coal and European merchandise; there were a few junks equipped for fishing, and a considerable flotilla of sampans with their parti-colored tents lay at anchor, rocked *by* the light lapping of the water. There was not a breath of air.

This quay was offensive to me. It was dirty arid battered, covered with black dust and strewn with the entrails of fish. The stench, the sound of quarreling, notes of a flute, and the barking of a dog came to us from within the hovels that flanked it lice-infested tea-houses, cutthroat shops, suspicious work stalls. Laughingly, Clara showed me a sort of little booth where, spread out on caladium leaves, they sold portions of rats and quartered dogs, rotten fish and emaciated chickens smeared with copal, bunches of bananas and bleeding bats, threaded on the same spit.

As we went on the stench became more unbearable and the filth thicker. On the stream the boats were jammed and huddled—a mass of sinister prows and miserable sail, torn to rags. A dense population lived here fishermen and pirates—frightful demons of the sea with wizened faces, lips reddened by the betel, and glances which made you shudder. They were playing dice, howling, and fighting; others, more peaceful, were gutting fish which they then strung in garlands and hung out in the sun to dry on ropes. Still others were training monkeys to perform a thousand tricks and obscenities.

"Amazing, isn't it?" Clara said to me. "And there are more than thirty thousand who have no other homes than their boats! The devil only knows how they manage!"

She lifted her dress, exposing the lower part of her lithe and agile leg, and for a long time we followed the horrible road, as far as the bridge which, with its bizarre superstructure and five massive arches painted in violent colors, straddled the stream at the mercy of the current and the eddies.

Upon the bridge the scene changed, but the odor grew stronger—that odor peculiar to all of China, and which in the cities, forests, and fields, makes you think constantly of decomposition and death.

Little shops built like pagodas, tents in the shape of kiosks draped with bright silky materials, immense parasols set up in chariots, baskets on wheels—all were crowded together. In these shops and under these tents and parasols fat merchants with bellies like hippopotami, clad in yellow, blue, and green robes, howling and tapping on gongs to attract customers, were hawking carcasses of all sorts: dead rats, drowned dogs, quartered deer and horses, purulent fowl, all piled pell-mell in broad bronze pans.

"Here, here, this way! Come this way! Look... and choose! You can find no better any place else. There is none rotten." And, delving into the basins, they brandished vile quarters of sanious meat like flags at the end of long iron-prongs, and with fierce grimaces accentuating the slashes of rouge on their faces painted like masks, amid the maddening reverberation of the gongs and the simultaneous uproar they repeated:

"Here, here, this way! Come this way. Look... and choose! You can find no better any place else. There is none rotten."

As soon as we had reached the bridge, Clara said to me:

"Now, you see, we're late. It's your fault! Let's hurry!"

In fact, a great crowd of Chinese women, and among them some English and Russian women—for there were only a very few men, except for the shopkeepers—was swarming on the bridge. Gowns embroidered with flowers and weird designs, variegated parasols, fans fluttering like birds, laughter, exclamations of joy and squabbling—all these vibrated, sang and hovered in the sunlight, like a celebration of life and love.

"Here, here, this way! Come this way!"

Bewildered by the jostling, deafened by the screeching of the merchants and the sonorous vibrations of the gongs. I almost had to fight to make a way through the throng and protect Clara from insults and blows. It was truly a grotesque combat, for I possessed no resistance or strength, and felt myself carried along by this human tumult as easily as a dead tree tumbled about in the furious waters of a torrent. Clara hurled herself into the thick of it with all her strength. She submitted to the brutal contact and, so to speak, the violation of this crowd, with passionate delight. Once she cried gloriously:

"Look, sweetheart! My dress is all torn. It's delicious!"

We had great difficulty in opening a passage to die booths, which were crowded and besieged as for a pillage.

"Look and choose! You can find no better any place else!"

"Here, here, this way! Right this way!"

Clara took the darling little pitchfork from the hands of the boy who was following us with her darling little basket, and she prodded about in the pans:

"You pick too... pick, sweetheart!"

I felt my heart would fail me, because of the appalling odor of the grave which was wafted from these booths... stirred-up pans... all this crowd rushing upon the corpses as though they were flowers.

"Clara... Clara!" I implored. "Let's go away, I beg you!"

"Oh, how pale you are! And why! Isn't it a lot of fun?"

"Clara, dear Clara!" I insisted, "I can't possibly stand this odor any longer."

"But it doesn't smell bad, my love. It smells of death, that's all."

She did not seem to be affected. No grimace of disgust wrinkled her white skin, fresh as a cherry blossom. From the veiled ardor of her eyes, from the fluttering of her nostrils, she seemed to be experiencing thrills of passion. She inhaled the stench with delight, like a perfume.

"Oh, he lovely... lovely piece!"

With graceful gestures, she filled the basket with the abominable scraps. And, painfully, through the excited crowd and amid the vile smells, we continued on our way.

"Quick! quick!"

PART 3

The Bangniois built on the bank of the river. Its quadrangular walls enclose more than a hundred thousand square meters of land. There isn't a single window, and no other opening than the immense door crowned by red dragons and fortified by heavy iron bars. The watchtowers, square towers surmounted by roofs with upturned edges, mark the four corners of the sinister battlements. Other smaller turrets are spaced between them at regular intervals. At night these towers are lit up like lighthouses, and cast around the bagnio, over the meadows and the stream, a revelatory light. One of the walls dips its solid foundations into the black, fetid, deep water, and is hung with slimy algae. By means of a drawbridge, a low door communicates with the stockade which extends to mid-stream and to whose piles many trade-junks and sampans are moored. Two spearmen, lance in hand, keep watch at the door! On the right of the stockade, a little cruiser, like our river patrol-boats, lies motionless, the mouths of its three cannons trained on the bagnio. On the left, as far as the eye can see along the river, twenty-five or thirty lines of boats mask the opposite shore with a jumble of variegated hulls, gaudy masts, rigging and grey sails. And from time to time, you can see those massive paddlewheel boats passing, propelled by wretches locked in a cage who painfully work them with their tense stiff arms.

Behind the bagnio, and as far as the mountain which girdles the horizon with a somber line, extend rocky, rolling fields, here dirty brown and there the color of dried blood, in which grow only scant acres, bluish thistles and stunted cherry trees that never bloom. Infinite desolation! Overwhelming misery! During eight months of the year the sky is blue—a blue washed with red in which the reflections of a perpetual fire glow—an implacable blue into which no chance cloud ever dares to venture. The sun parches the earth, bakes the rocks, and vitrifies the pebbles which burst underfoot with the crunching of glass and the crackling of flame. No bird defies this aerial furnace. Only invisible organisms live there—clumps of bacilli which, toward evening, when the bleak mists rise with the chant of the sailors on the sluggish stream, distinctly assume the shapes of fever, pestilence, and death. What a contrast with the other shore, where the fat, rich soil covered, with gardens and orchards, nourishes giant trees and marvelous flowers!

On the other side of the bridge we luckily found a palanquin, \which carried us across the scorching fields almost to the bagnio, whose doors were still closed. A squad of police, armed with lances and yellow pennants, with great shields which almost covered them, held back the huge impatient crowd, which was swelling every minute. There were rows of tents where people were drinking tea, munching pretty bonbons and rose—or acacia—petals rolled in a fine scented paste sprinkled with sugar. In others, musicians played the flute and poets recited verses, while the *punka,* fanning the torrid air, produced a slight breeze which cooled their faces. Strolling merchants sold images, stories of famous crimes, models of torture and martyrdom, prints and ivories, curiously obscene. Clara bought one of the latter, and said to me:

"You can see that the Chinese, who are accused of being barbarians, are, to the contrary, more civilized than we; for they are grounded deeper in the logic of life and the harmony of nature! They do not consider the act of love a shameful thing that should be hidden. To the contrary, they glorify it, hymning all the gestures and caresses; just like the ancients, moreover, for whom the sexual organ, far from being an object of infamy and an image of impurity, was a God! You see how all Occidental art loses by the fact that the magnificent expressions of love have been denied it. With us, eroticism is poor, stupid and frigid. It is always presented in ambiguous attitudes of sin, while here it preserves all its vital scope, all its passionate poetry and the stupendous pulse of all nature. But you are only a European lover... a poor, timid, chilly little soul, in whom Catholicism has stupidly inculcated a fear of nature and a hatred of love. It has warped and perverted the sense of life in you."

"Dear Clara," I objected, "is it really natural for you to seek sensuality in decomposition, and urge Your desires to greater heights by horrible spectacles of suffering and death? Isn't that, to the contrary, a perversion of that nature whose cult you invoke, in order perhaps to excuse whatever criminal and monstrous qualities your sensuality involves?"

"No!" said Clara, quickly, "since love and death are the same thing! And since decomposition is the eternal resurrection of life... Look—" Suddenly she interrupted herself, and said:

"But why do you tell me that? You're funny!" And with a charming pout, she added:

"How provoking that you don't understand anything! How is it you don't feel it? How is it you haven't already felt that it is—I don't even say by love, but by the heightened sensuality which is the perfection of love—that all the intellectual faculties of man awaken and become more acute? And it's by this sensuality alone that you attain the full development of personality. Look! In the act of love, have you ever thought, for instance, of committing a beautiful crime? That is to say, lifting yourself above social prejudices and all the laws—above everything, in fact? And if you haven't thought if it, then why do you bother making love?"

"I haven't the strength to argue," I stammered, "and it seems to me we are walking in a nightmare. This sun... this crowd... these smells... and your eyes—ah, your torturous and lustful eyes—and your voice... and your penchant for crime... all that terrifies me, and it's all driving me mad!"

Clara gave a little mocking laugh.

"Poor little pet!" she sighed, comically. "You won't say that tonight, when you're in my arms... and when I love you!"

The crowd was growing more and more restless. Bonzes crouched under parasols, laid out long red gowns, like pools of blood, struck frenzied blows on gongs and hurled gross invectives at the passers—by who, to counteract their curses, devoutly threw large pieces of change into metal bowls.

Clara led me into a tent all embroidered with peach flowers, made me sit down by her on a pile of cushions, and stroking my forehead with her exciting hand— with her hand which dispensed forgetfulness and intoxication, she said to me:

"My God, how long it takes, darling! Every week it's the same thing. They take so long to open the door. Why don't you speak? Do I frighten you? Are you glad you came? Are you happy to have me caress you, dear beloved little rascal? Oh, your beautiful tired eyes! It's the fever—and it's me too! Say it's me. Do you Want to drink some tea? Do you want another hamamelis tablet?"

"I'd rather not stay here longer! I'd rather sleep." "Sleep! How strange you are. Oh, you'll see how beautiful it is! And what extraordinary... what Unknown... what marvelous desires it instills into Your flesh! We'll come back by the river, in my sampan. And we'll spend the night in a flower-boat. Wouldn't you like to?" She lightly tapped my hands several times with her fan.

"But you're not listening to me! Why aren't you listening to me? You're pale and melancholy. And, really, you're not listening to me at all." She snuggled up against me, sinuous and caressing:

"You're not listening to me, wretch," she went on. "And you don't even caress me! Caress me, darling! Feel how cold and firm my breasts are." And, in a hollow voice, her eyes darting green, voluptuous and cruel flames, she spoke like this.

"Listen! Eight days ago I saw an extraordinary thing. Oh, dear love, I saw a man whipped for stealing a fish. The judge simply said this: 'One must not always say of a man who carries a fish in his hand: He is a fisherman'! And he sentenced the man to die under the iron rods. For a fish, darling! It took place in the torture-garden. The man was kneeling on the ground—imagine it—and his head rested on a sort of block... a block all black with old blood. His back and loins were bare; a back and loins like old gold! I arrived just at the moment when a soldier, having gripped his queue, which was very long, was knotting it to a ring riveted in a stone slab in the ground. Beside the culprit, another soldier was heating a little... a very little iron switch, at the fire of a forge. And then—pay attention to me! Are you listening? When the switch was red, the soldier whipped the man on the loins. The switch hissed in the air, and it penetrated far into the muscles, which crackled, and a little reddish steam arose... you understand? Then the soldier let the switch cool in the flesh, which bubbled up and closed over it. Then, when it was cold, he violently jerked it out with a single movement, along with little bleeding bits. And the man hurled frightful cries of agony. Then the soldier began again. He did it fifteen times! And I too, darling—it seemed to me that with every blow, the switch entered my loins. It was fierce and very sweet!"

As I was silent:

"It was fierce and very sweet," she repeated. "If you knew how handsome that man was... how strong he was! Muscles like those of a statue. Kiss me, darling... kiss me!"

Clara's pupils had rolled back. Between her half closed lids I could see nothing but the whites of her eyes. Again she spoke:

"He did not budge. It made little waves on his back. Oh, your lips!"

After some seconds of silence, she went on:

"Last year, with Annie, I saw something much more astonishing: I saw a man who had attacked his mother and then disemboweled her with a knife. It seemed, besides, that he was crazy. He was sentenced to the torture of the caress. Yes, my darling. Isn't it wonderful? Strangers aren't allowed to witness that torture, which, besides, is very rare today. But we gave some money to the guard, who hid us behind a screen. Annie and I saw everything! The madman—he didn't seem to be mad—was stretched out on a very low table, his limbs and body were tied by stout ropes, and his mouth was gagged, so he couldn't make movement or utter a cry. A woman with a grave face, not beautiful, not young, and dressed entirely in black, her bare arm circled by a broad gold band, came and kneeled beside the madman. She grasped him and set about her task. Oh darling, darling, if you could have seen! It lasted four hours... four hours, think of it! Four hours of frightful and skilled caresses, during which the woman's hand did not relax a moment, during which her face remained cold and gloomy! The culprit died in a jet of blood, which splattered the entire face of the tormentress. Never have I seen anything so atrocious; and it was so atrocious, my darling, that both Annie and I fainted. I still think of it!"

With an air of regret, she added:

"On one of her fingers that woman had a huge ruby which, during the torture, flashed in the sunlight like a little red dancing flame. Annie bought it, but I don't know what became of it. I'd like very much to have it."

Clara was silent, her mind having undoubtedly returned to the bloody image of that abominable memory.

Some minutes later a murmur ran through the tents and the crowd. Through my heavy eyelids which despite me had almost closed at the horror of this tale, I saw gown after gown passing, and parasols, and fans, and happy faces, and accursed faces, dancing, whirling, rushing. It was like a burst of immense flowers, like a whirl of fantastic birds.

"The doors, darling," cried Clara, "the doors are being opened! Come, come quickly! And don't be sad any more. Ah, I beg you! Think of all the beautiful things you're going to see, and the ones I told you about!"

I got up... and seizing my arm, she dragged me along, I know not where.

PART 4

The door to the Bagnio opened on a wide, dark corridor. Through the corridor, but from beyond, there came to us the sound of a bell, muffled and deadened by the distance. And hearing it, Clara joyfully clapped her hands.

"Oh, darling! The bell! The bell! We're in luck. Don't be unhappy any more... don't be ill any more, I beg you!"

The crowd was milling so furiously at the entrance of the bagnio that the police had great difficulty in bringing about a little order in the tumult. It was into this crush of cackling, shouting, and suffocating people into this rubbing of cloth against cloth, and jostling, of parasols and fans, that Clara resolutely hurled her self, exalted by the ringing of the bell. I had not thought of asking her why it was ringing like that, or the meaning of its muffled distant tolling, which caused her so much pleasure.

"The bell! The bell! The bell! Come!"

But we couldn't get very far despite the efforts of the boys carrying baskets who, thrusting out violently with their elbows, were attempting to make way for their mistresses. Tall porters with grimacing faces, frightfully emaciated, their chests bare and scarred beneath their rags, were holding baskets of meat above their heads, in which the sun was accelerating decomposition and hatching swarm of maggots. They were specters of crime and famine, images of nightmare and massacre, demons materialized from the darkest and most terrifying legends of China.

Nearby I saw one whose laugh exposed a slash of saw-toothed mouth with its betel-lacquered teeth, and extended to the edge of his billy-goat beard, sinister and distorted. Some were cursing and cruelly pulling each others queues; others, with the gliding movements of felines, were slipping through the human thicket, picking pockets, cutting purses, snatching jewels and then disappearing with their loot.

"The bell! The bell!" repeated Clara.

"But what bell?"

"You'll see. It's a surprise!"

And the smells that arose from the crowd—smells of the latrine and the slaughter-house, the stink of corpses and the perfumes of living flesh—nauseated me and chilled me to the marrow. I felt the same lethargic sensation I had so often experienced in the forests of Annam, in the evening, when the miasma rose from the deepest leaf—mold and death lurked behind every flower, every leaf, and every blade of grass. At the same time, shoved and jostled from every side, my breath almost failing, I was finally at the point of fainting. "Clara! Clara!" I called.

She made me breathe salts, whose cordial power restored me a little. She was unrestrained and delighted in the midst of this crowd whose odor she inhaled, and to whose repugnant embraces she submitted with a sort of swooning lust. She offered her body—all her lithe and vibrant body—to the brutality, the blows, and the clawing. Her white skin was now a glowing pink; her eyes reflected a languid thrill of sensual delight; her lips were swollen, like firm buds ready to blossom. Once more, with a sort of mocking pity, she said to me:

"Ah, little woman! little woman... little woman! You'll never be anything but a little, insignificant woman!"

Coming from the dazzling and blinding light of the sun, the corridor which we finally reached seemed at first full of shadow. Then little by little the shadows faded away, and I could get a clear idea of where I was.

The passageway was vast and lit from above by windows which only allowed an attenuated light to pass through their opaque glass. The cool and moist air, almost cold, wrapped me from head to foot, like the breath of a woodland spring. The walls sweated like the galleries of a subterranean grotto. Under my feet, burned by the pebbles of the field, the sand which covered the flags of the tunnel possessed the gentle softness of seaside dunes. I breathed the air deeply, with full lungs. Clara said to me:

"You see how nice they are to the convicts here. At least they're cool."

"But where are they?" I asked. "I can see nothing but walls on either side." Clara smiled.

"How strange you are! Here you are more impatient than I! Wait... wait a little! In a minute, darling. Listen!"

She halted and pointed out a vague spot in the tunnel, her eyes more brilliant, her nostrils palpitating, her ears attentive to sound, like a doe at bay in the forest.

"Do you hear? There they are! Do you hear?"

Then, from beyond the murmur of the crowd which thronged the passageway, from beyond the hum of voices, I perceived cries, hollow moans, the dragging of chains, breaths panting like a forge—a strange and prolonged growling of beasts. It seemed to come from the depths of the wall, from below the ground, from the very abyss of death. You could not tell whence.

"Do you hear?" Clara went on. "There they are... you'll see them in a minute... let's go! Take my arm. Watch out... there they are! There they are!" We started to walk again, followed by the boy who was attentive to the gestures of his mistress. And the frightful corpse-odor also accompanied us, no longer left us, and was augmented by other odors whose ammoniacal acridity stung our eyes—and throats.

The bell still rang down there—far off—slow and soft, muffled, like the cry of a man in agony. For the third time Clara repeated:

"Oh, that bell! He's dying, he's dying, my darling. Perhaps we'll see him!"

Suddenly I felt her fingers clenched tensely in my flesh.

"Darling! darling! On your right! How horrible!"

Swiftly, I turned my head. The infernal procession had begun. In the wall at the right there were vast cells, or rather cages, enclosed by bars and separated from each other by thick stone partitions. The first ten were each occupied by ten condemned men; and all ten offered the same spectacle. Their necks were clasped in a pillory so wide it was impossible to see their bodies, and you'd have thought they were frightful severed living heads placed on tables. Crouched amid their filth, their hands and feet chained, they could neither stretch nor lie down, nor even take a rest. The slightest movement displaced the iron collars about their bare throats and bleeding necks, and made them utter howls of pain, alternately interspersed with fierce insults to us and supplications to the gods. I was mute with horror.

Deftly, with pretty shivers and exquisite gestures, Clara prodded in the boy's basket, and lifted out some small scraps of meat, which she gracefully tossed through the bars of the cage. Ten heads simultaneously turned in their balanced collars; simultaneously, twenty bulging eyeballs cast inflamed glances at the meat—glances of terror and hunger. Then one cry of agony arose from the ten contorted mouths. And, conscious of their impotence, the condemned men did not move again. They remained with their heads slightly inclined as though ready to roll down the slope of the collar, their pale and fleshless features convulsed in a rigid grimace, in a sort of frozen leer.

"They can't eat," Clara explained. "They can't reach the meat. Naturally, in such contraptions, it's understandable. After all, it's not very new. It's the torture of Tantalus, redoubled by the horror of the Chinese imagination, eh? Would you believe there were such unhappy people in the world?"

Again she cast through the bars a small bit of carcass which, falling on the edge of one of the collars, made it sway slightly. Hollow groans were the answer to this gesture; a fiercer and more desperate hatred lit up the twenty eyeballs at the same time. Instinctively, Clara recoiled:

"You see," she continued in a less assured tone, "it amuses them for me to give them meat. It helps these poor devils pass the time... it provides them with a little illusion. Come along... come along!"

We passed slowly before the ten cages. Women standing before them shouted, or uttered bursts of laughter, or abandoned themselves to impassioned mimicry. I saw a very blond, Russian woman with a cold, limpid glance, hold out to the sufferers a vile greenish mess, which she alternately extended and withdrew on the tip of her parasol. Baring their fangs like mad dogs, with starving expressions which no longer expressed anything human, they tried to snatch the food which always escaped their sticky, slavering mouths. Curious women watched with attentive and joyful faces all the moves of this cruel game.

"What whores!" said Clara, seriously indignant. "Really, there are some women who have no respect for anything. It's shameful!"

I asked:

"What crimes have these creatures committed, to suffer such torment?" She replied carelessly:

"I don't know. Nothing, perhaps, or doubtless very little. Petty thefts from shopkeepers, I suppose. Besides, they are only common people... wharf-rats... vagabonds... paupers! They don't interest me very much. But there are others. You'll see my poet in a minute. Yes, I have a favorite here, and he's actually a poet! Isn't it funny? Ah, but he's a great poet, you know! He composed an admirable satire against a prince who had robbed the treasury. And he detests the English.

"One evening two years ago he was brought to my house. He sang delightful things. But he excelled especially in satire. You'll see him. He's the handsomest... at least if he's not dead already! You see, in this regime nothing is astonishing. What annoys me most is that he doesn't recognize me any more. I talk to him... I sing his poems to him... and he no longer recognizes them. It's really horrible, don't you think? Bah! It s also funny, after all!"

She tried to be gay, but her gaiety sounded false. Her face was grave; her nostrils palpitated faster. She leaned on my arm more heavily, and I felt shivers run all through her body.

Then I noticed that in the left wall, opposite each cell, deep niches had been cut which contained painted and sculptured wood which, with the frightful realism peculiar to the art of the Far. East, represented every species of torture in use in China: scenes of decapitation, strangulation, flaying and tearing of flesh... demoniacal and mathematical conceptions which pushed the science of torture to a refinement unknown to our Occidental cruelty, inventive as it is. It was a museum of horror and despair, where no human ferocity had been overlooked, and which every minute of the day ceaselessly recalled to the convicts, by precise imagery, the skilful death to which their executioners destined them.

"Don't look at that!" Clara said with a pout of disgust. "They're only painted wood, my love. Look this way, where it's real—Look! There's my poet—right there!" And she halted abruptly before his cage.

Pale, fleshless, slashed with a skeletal grin, its cheek bones bursting the gangrenous skin, its jaws bare beneath the flaps of its trembling lips—a face was pressed against the bars, between two long, bony hands, like the dry feet of a bird. That face, from which every trace of humanity had disappeared forever; those bleeding eyes, and those hands, now scabby claws, terrified me. I backed up with an instinctive movement, to escape the feel of the pestilential breath of that mouth against my skin, and to avoid the scratch of those claws. But Clara quickly led me back before the cage. In its depths, in ominous shadow, five living beings who had once been men, were walking and walking, and turning and turning, their torsos bare, their skulls black with dried, blood-streaked wounds. Panting, barking, howling, they vainly tried to shake the solid stone of the partition by pushing violently against it. Then they started to walk and turn again, with the suppleness of beasts and the obscenities of monkeys. A wide, transverse partition hid the lower part of their bodies, and from the invisible floor of the cell a suffocating, deadly stench arose.

"Good-day, poet!" said Clara, addressing the Face. "I'm nice, eh? I've come to see you once again, poor dear man! Do you recognize me today? No? Why don't you recognize me? I'm still beautiful, and I loved you a whole night!"

The Face did not budge. Its eyes never left the meat basket the boy was carrying. And from its throat there came a raucous, bestial sound.

"Are you hungry?" Clara continued. "I'll give you something to eat. I've chosen the best piece at the market for you. But, first, would you like me to recite Your poem: *The Three Mistresses?* Would you? You'll enjoy hearing it." And she recited:

I have three mistresses.
The first has a spirit mobile as a bamboo leaf.
Her light and Playful spirit is like the feathery blossom of the eulalia.
Her eye is like the lotus.
And her beast is as firm as the lemon.
Her hair, twisted in a single braid, falls over her golden shoulder like a black serpent.
Her voice has the sweetness of mountain honey.
Her loins are slender and lithe.
Her thighs are round as the supple trunk of the banana-tree.
Her gait is that of a young and playful elephant.
She loves passion, knows how to give it birth and vary it!

I have three mistresses.

Clara interrupted herself:

"Don't you remember?" she asked, "don't you love my voice any more?"

The Face had not budged. It seemed not to hear. Its eyes still devoured the horrible basket, and its tongue clacked in its mouth, wet with saliva.

"Come," said Clara. "Listen again! And you'll eat, since you're so hungry." And in a slow and rhythmic voice she continued:

I have three mistresses.

The second has abundant hair which gleams and flows in long silky garlands.

Her glance would disturb the God of Love.

And make the wagtail blush.

The body of that graceful woman flows like a golden vine.

Her earrings are encrusted with precious stones.

Like a flower jeweled with frost on a cold and sunny morning.

Her clothes are summer gardens.

And temples on festival-days.

And her firm, full breasts shine like a pair of golden vases

Filled with intoxicating liquors and perfumes.

I have three mistresses.

"Ouah! ouah!" barked the Face, while in the cage the five other condemned creatures echoed the sinister bark, walking and walking, turning and turning... Clara continued:

I have three mistresses.

The hair of the third is plaited,

And rolled about her head.

And never has known the sweetness of perfumed oils.

That face which mirrors passion is deformed,

Her body is like a pig's.

You'd say she was always angry.

She always scolds and complains.

Her breasts and belly exhale a fishy odor.

She is ill-favored in her entire person.

She eats everything and drinks to excess.

And her wan eyes are always bleary.

And her bed is more repugnant than a lapwing's nest.

And she is the one I love.

And I love her because there is something more mysteriously attractive than beauty: it is corruption.

Corruption in which the eternal heat of life resides,

In which the eternal renewal of metamorphoses unfolds!

I *have three mistresses...* The poem was ended. Clara was silent. Its eyes avidly fixed upon the basket, the Face had not ceased barking during the recitation of the last stanza. Then, addressing me sadly, Clara said:

"You see, he doesn't remember anything any more! He has lost the memory of his verses, like my face. And that mouth I kissed no longer knows the words of mankind! It's really unheard of!"

From the basket of meat she chose the best and thickest piece, and her body prettily thrust forward, she held it out at the tip of her pitchfork, to the fleshless Face whose eyes glowed like two little braziers.

"Eat, poor poet!" she said. "Now eat"

With the motions of a starved beast, the poet seized the horrible stinking scrap in his claws and carried it to his mouth where, for a moment, I saw it hanging like a piece of filth from the streets, between the fangs of a dog. But immediately, in the shaking cage, there was roaring and pouncing. Nothing could be seen but bare torsos, mingled and clasped to each other, grasped by long, thin arms, torn by jaws and claws, and contorted faces tearing at the meat. I could see nothing more. And I heard the noise of struggle on the floor of the cage, chests panting and wheezing with raucous respiration, the thumping fall of bodies, scuffling of flesh, cracking of bones, the muffled shocks of carnage, and a rattling of throats! From time to time a face appeared above the partition with the prey in its teeth, then disappeared. More barking, more rattling in their throats, and then silence—then nothing! Clara clung to me, trembling.

"Ah, my darling... my darling!" I cried to her:

"Throw them all the meat. You see they're killing each other." She clasped me, embraced me.

"Kiss me. Caress me... It's horrible! It's too horrible!" And lifting herself up to my lips, she said, in a fierce kiss:

"I can't hear anything. They're dead. Do you think they're all dead?"

When we lifted our eyes to the cage again, a fleshless and bloody Face was pressed between the bars and was looking at us steadily, almost proudly. A strip of meat hung from its lips, amid threads of purple slaver. Its chest heaved. Clara applauded, her voice still trembling.

"It's he! It's my poet! He's the strongest!" She threw him all the meat in the basket, and with her throat tightening:

"I'm stifling," she said. "And you too—you're all pale, my love. Let's breathe the air in the Torture Garden for a little while."

Slight drops of perspiration beaded her forehead. She wiped them away, and turning to the poet, she spoke, accompanying her words with a slight gesture of her ungloved hand:

"I'm happy you were the strongest today! Eat! Eat! I'll come to see you again. Good-bye."

She dismissed the boy who now was no longer needed. We went up the middle of the corridor with a hurried step, despite the hindrance of the crowd, careful to

avoid looking to the right or left. The bell still rang. But its vibrations were diminishing, diminishing so that they were no more than the breath of a breeze, a tiny
infant's cry, smothered behind a curtain.

"What does that bell mean? Where does it come from?" I asked.

"What? Don't you know? Why, it's the bell in the Torture Garden! Imagine...
They bind a victim, and they lay him under the bell. Then they ring it wildly until
the vibration kills him! And when death is near, they ring it gently, gently, so it
doesn't come too soon—like they're doing down there, now! Do you hear?" I was
going to speak, but Clara closed my mouth with a tap of her unfolded fan.

"Now be quiet! Don't say anything! And listen, my love. And think what a dreadful death they must bring—those vibrations beneath the bell. And come with me.
And say nothing... nothing."

When we came out of the corridor, the bell was no more than the drone of an
insect... a rustling of wings, scarcely perceptible in the distance.

PART 5

In the center of the prison, the Torture Garden occupies an immense quadrilat-
eral space, enclosed by walls whose stones can no longer be seen because of a
thick covering of tangled shrubs and climbing plants. It was built towards the
middle of the last century by Li-Pe-Hang, superintendent of the imperial gardens
and the cleverest botanist China ever had. In the stacks of the Musee Guimet you
may consult many works which celebrate his fame, and very curious prints in
which his most illustrious works are set forth. The wonderful Kew Gardens—the
only ones in Europe which satisfy us—owe much to him from a technical point
of view, and also from the point of view of floral ornamentation and landscape
gardening, but they are still a far cry from the pure beauty of the Chinese model.
According to Clara, that exquisite attraction is lacking which is implied by the
mingling of torture with horticulture, blood with flowers.

The earth, composed of sand and pebbles, like all that barren terrain, was largely dug up and reworked with virgin soil brought at great expense from the other
side of the river. It is related that more than thirty thousand coolies perished of
fever in the construction of this gigantic garden, which took twenty-two years.
These hecatombs were far from being useless. Mingled with the soil as fertiliz-
er—for they were buried on the spot the dead enriched it by their slow decomposition, and besides, in no other place, even in the heart of the most fantastic tropical jungles, could a land richer in natural mould be found. Its extraordinary fer-
tility, far from being exhausted in the end, still operates today through the excre-
ment of the prisoners, the blood of the tortured, and all the organic debris the
crowd deposits there every week which, carefully collected and cleverly rendered
with the daily corpses in special retting vats, forms a potent compost for which
plants are greedy and which makes them more vigorous and beautiful. Forks of
the river, ingeniously diverted through the garden according to the requirements
of the vegetation, provide a permanent moisture, and at the same time serve to fill

the pools and canals, whose water is thus constantly renewed, and in which almost extinct zoological forms are conserved—among others, the famous fish with six humps, celebrated by Yu-Sin and our compatriot, the poet Robert de Montesquiou.

The Chinese are incomparable gardeners, quite superior to our vulgar horticulturists, who only attempt to destroy the beauty of plants by disrespectful practices and criminal hybridizations. The latter are actual malefactors, and I cannot imagine why very drastic penal laws have not already been passed against them, in the name of all life. I should even be happy to see them mercilessly guillotined, in preference to those anemic assassins whose social 'selectivism' is much more laudable and generous, since, the majority of the time, it only singles out very ugly old ladies and vile bourgeois, who are a perpetual outrage to life. Besides having pushed their infamy to the point of deforming the touching beauty of simple flowers, our gardeners have dared to perpetrate that degrading joke of giving to the fragility of roses, to the star like rays of the clematis, to the heavenly glory of the larkspur, to the heraldic mystery of the iris and to the modesty of the violet—the names of old generals and disgraced politicians. In our flower-beds it is not rare to encounter an iris, for instance, baptized: *General Archinard!* There are narcissi—narcissi!—grotesquely designated: *The Triumph of President Felix Faure;* hollyhocks which, without protesting, accept the ridiculous appellation of: *Mourning for Monsieur Thiers;* violets—timid, sensitive and exquisite violets, to whom the names of *General Skobeleff* and *Admiral Avellan* have not seemed insulting nicknames! Flowers—all beauty, light and joy—all tenderness too, evoking the fierce mustachios and heavy riding-breeches of a soldier, or the parliamentary top-knot of a minister! Flowers mixing with political opinions and serving to spread electoral propaganda! To what aberrations and intellectual degeneration might such blasphemies and attempts at the divinity of things correspond? If it were possible that a being so stripped of a soul felt a hatred for flowers, European, and particularly French, gardeners would amply prove this inconceivably sacrilegious paradox!

Being perfect artists and ingenuous poets, the Chinese have piously preserved the love and holy cult of flowers; one of the very rare and most ancient traditions which has survived their decadence. And since flowers had to be distinguished from each other, they have attributed graceful analogies to them, dreamy images, pure and passionate names which perpetuate and harmonize in our minds the sensations of gentle charm and violent intoxication with which they inspire us. So it is that certain peonies, their favorite flower, are saluted by the Chinese, according to their form or color, by these delicious names, each an entire poem and an entire novel: *The Young Girl Who Offers Her Breasts,* or: *The Water That Sleeps Beneath the Moon,* or: *The Sunlight in the Forest, or: The First Desire of the Reclining Virgin,* or: *My Gown Is No Longer All White Because in Tearing It the Son of Heaven Left a Little Rosy Stain;* or, even better, this one: I *Possessed My*

Lover in the Garden.

And Clara who told me all these charming things, cried indignantly and stamped on the ground with her little feet, shod in yellow leather:

"And they treat these divine poets, who call their flowers *I Possessed My Lover in the Garden,* like lice and savages!"

The Chinese are rightfully proud of the Torture Garden, the most thoroughly beautiful perhaps in all China, where, moreover, marvelous gardens are common. Here are gathered the rarest species of their flora, the most delicate as well as the hardiest, those which come from the snow-line on the mountains, or sprout in the burning furnace of the meadows, and also those, mysterious and fierce, which are hidden in the most impenetrable jungles, and to which popular superstition has given the names of evil genii. From the mangrove to the saxatile azalea, from the horned and biflorous violet to the distillating nepenthe, from the volubilate hibiscus to the stoloniferous helianthus, from the androsace, invisible in its rocky fissure, to the most wildly twining liana, each specie is represented by numerous specimens which, gorged with organic nourishment and treated according to the proper formula by clever gardeners, take on abnormal forms and colorations, whose prodigious intensity we have difficulty in imagining in our gloomy climate and our uninspired gardens.

In the hollow of a valley from which a number of sinuous alleys and paths branch out bordered by flowers in a supple and harmoniously flowing design, a vast pool crossed by the arch of a wooden bridge painted bright green, marks the center of the garden. White water lilies and nelumbos brighten its surface with their trailing leaves and floating corollas—yellow, mauve, white, rose and purple. Tufts of iris lift their slender stalks, on whose tops strange, symbolic birds seem to perch; and plumed rushes, galingales like hair, and giant luzula: mingle their incongruous leafage with the phalliform and vulvoid clusters of the most stupefying arum-lilies.

On the edge of the pool, by an inspired calculation, amid the plaited hart's-tongue, globe-flowers and inulre, artistically trimmed glycines rise and arch over the water, which reflects their blue, swaying clusters. And pearl-grey cranes with silky plumes and scarlet wattles, white herons and white storks with Manchurian blue necks, stalk about amid the high grass with indolent grace and sacerdotal majesty.

Here and there on little hillocks and red rocks covered with dwarf ferns, androsace, saxifrage and creeping shrubs, slim and graceful kiosks lift above the bamboos and the dwarf cedars the pointed cones of their gilded roofs, and the delicate ribs of their framework whose extremities curve inward and up with a bold movement. Along the slopes, every species swarms: epimedia issuing from among the stones, with its frail flowers stirring and fluttering like insects; orange hemerocallis offering its calyx of a day to the hawk—moth and white renothera offering its calyx of an hour; fleshy opuntia, eomecons, morrea, and sheets, streams, and brooklets of primroses—those Chinese primroses which are so extremely polymorphous, and of which we possess only poverty-stricken images in our hot-houses. And there were so many charming and bizarre forms, and so many blending colors: and around the kiosks, between the patches of lawn, in the tremulous distance, it was like a rosy, mauve, and white rain, a variegated shimmering, a pearly, pink, and milky pulsation so tender and changing that it is impossible for me to express in words its infinite sweetness and ineffable idyllic poetry.

How had we come there? I knew nothing of it. Under Clara's hand a door had suddenly opened in the walls of the dark corridor. And suddenly, as though by the influence of a fairy wand, I was flooded with celestial light, and before me there were horizons and horizons!

I gazed, dazzled; dazzled by the softer light, the gentler sky, dazzled even by the great blue shadows that the trees laid softly upon the grass, like voluptuous rugs; dazzled by the touching magic of the flowers and the floors of peonies that the slight shelter of the reeds shielded from the mortal heat of the sun. On one of the lawns, not far from *us,* a sprinkler sprayed water in which all the colors of the rainbow played, and through which the grass and flowers took on the translucence of precious stones.

I gazed greedily, never tiring. But then I did not see all those details which I reconstructed later; I saw only an ensemble of mysteries and beauties whose sudden and consoling apparition I did not attempt to explain to myself. No more did I wonder whether it was reality that surrounded me, or only a dream. I wondered about nothing, thought of nothing, said nothing. Clara talked and talked. Doubtless she was still telling me story after story. I wasn't listening to her, nor did I feel her at my side. At that moment, her presence beside me was so far from me! And her voice was so far away, and so strange. Little by little, I finally regained my self-possession, my memories, and a perception of the realities of things, and I understood why and how I happened to be there.

Emerging from inferno, still pale from the horror of those faces of the damned, my nostrils still filled with the odor of decomposition and death, and my ears still humming with the howls of torture, the sight of this garden brought me sudden relaxation, after an exaltation and an unreal ascension of my entire being towards a dazzling land of dream. With delight, I drew in great gulps of the new air so impregnated with so many fine and soft aromas. It was the inexpressible joy of awakening after an oppressing nightmare. I tasted that ineffable impression of freedom which a man might feel who, having been buried alive in a frightful charnel house, has just lifted its stone and been resurrected to the sunlight with his flesh intact, his limbs freed, and his soul reborn.

A bench made of bamboo trunks was close by in the shadow of an immense ash whose purple leaves sparkled in the sun, creating the illusion of a dome of rubies. I sat down, or rather, I let myself fall back, for the joy of all this splendid life almost made me faint with an unsuspected passion.

And at my left I saw a Buddha, the stone guardian of this garden, squatting on his rock and displaying his tranquil face—his face of sovereign kindness, bathed in azure and sunlight. Sheaves of flowers and baskets of fruit covered the pedestal of the statue with propitiatory and perfumed offerings. A young girl in a yellow dress reached up to the forehead of the inexorable god, and piously crowned it with lotus and lady-slipper. Swallows swooped about, uttering little joyful squeaks. Then I thought-and with what religious enthusiasm and mystic adoration!—of the sublime life of him who, long before our Christ, had preached purity to men, and enunciation, and love.

But, hovering over me like sin itself, Clara, her mouth red, and like the flower of the cydonia, Clara with her green eyes, the grey-green of the young fruit of the almond tree, hastened to lead me back to reality, and, indicating the garden with a broad gesture, she said:

"See, my love, what marvelous artists the Chinese are, and how they contrive to make nature an accomplice of the refinement of their cruelty! In our frightful Europe which, for so long a time has not known what beauty is, they torture in secret, in the depths of their jails, or in public squares, among the vile drunken crowds. Here, it's among flowers, amid the prodigious enchantment and prodigious silence of all the flowers, that the instruments of torture are erected, the stake, the scaffold and the cross. You'll see them right away, so intimately mingled with the splendor of this floral orgy and the harmony of this unique and magical nature, that they seem in some way to merge with her, and be the miraculous flowers of this soil and this light." And, as I could not suppress a gesture of impatience:

"Silly!" said Clara. "Little fool! You don't understand anything!" Her forehead barred by a hard shadow, she continued:

"Come! Have you ever been at a festival when you were sad or ill? Well, then you've felt how much your sadness was irritated and exasperated, as by an insult, by the joyful faces and the beauty of things. It's an intolerable feeling. Think of what it must mean to a victim who is going to die under torture. Think how much the torture is multiplied in his flesh and his soul by all the splendor which surrounds him; and how much more atrocious is his agony, how much more hopelessly atrocious, darling!"

"I was thinking of love," I replied in a tone of reproach, "and here you are talking to me again—forever—about torture!"

"Doubtless! since it's the same thing—"

She had been standing beside me, her hands on my shoulder. And the red shadow of the ash wrapped her in a fiery glow. She sat down on the bench and continued:

"—and, since there are tortures wherever there are men, I can't do anything about it, my baby, and I try to adjust myself to it and enjoy it, for blood is a precious auxiliary of desire. It's the wine of love." With the tip of her parasol, she traced some naively indecent figures in the sand, and she said:

"I'm sure you think the Chinese crueler than we. No... not at all! We English? Ah, don't mention it! And you French? In your Algeria, in the confines of the desert, I saw this: One day some soldiers captured some Arabs; poor Arabs who had committed no other crime than to try to escape the brutality of their conquerors. The Colonel commanded them to be put to death immediately, without an inquiry, without a trial. And this is what happened: There were thirty of them. They dug thirty holes in the sand, and they buried them up to their necks, naked, with their heads shaved, in the noonday sun. So they wouldn't die too fast they watered them from time to time, like cabbages. At the end of an hour their eyelids were swollen, their eyes bulged from their sockets, their swollen tongues filled their mouths, which gaped frightfully, and their skin cracked and roasted on their skulls. It was unimaginative, I assure you, and even devoid of terror—those thirty dead heads, sticking out of the sand like shapeless rocks! And we! It's still worse! Ah, I remember the strange sensation I felt when, at Kandy, the gloomy former capital of Ceylon, I went up the steps of the temple where the English had stupidly, without torture, slaughtered the little Modeliar princes who, legends tell us, were so charming... like those skillfully made Chinese ikons, with so hieratically calm and pure of grace, and their golden halos and their long hands pressed together. I felt that what had happened there on those sacred steps, still uncleansed of that blood by eighty years of violent possession—was something more horrible than a human massacre; the destruction of a precious, touching and innocent beauty. The traces of that double European barbarity may be found at every step you take on the ancestral soil of that suffering and always mysterious India. The boulevards of Calcutta, the cool Himalayan villas in Darjeeling, the tribades of Benares and the sumptuous homes of the contractors in Bombay have not been able to efface the impression of mourning and death left everywhere by the atrocity of unskillful massacre, vandalism and senseless destruction. To the contrary, they accentuate it. No matter in what place it appears, civilization displays that face which bears the double imprint of sterile blood and ruins forever dead. Like Attila, it might say: 'Grass no longer grows where my horse has trod.' Look here, before you and around you! There is not a grain of sand that has not been bathed in blood, and what is that grain of sand itself, if not the dust of death? But how rich this blood is, and how fertile is the dust! Look... the grass is thick... flowers swarm everywhere and love is everywhere!"

Clara's face became exalted. A gentle melancholy softened the bar of shadow across her forehead and veiled the green flames of her eyes. She continued:

"Ah, how sad and poignant the little dead city Kandy seemed to me that day! In the torrid heat, a heavy silence hovered over it, and vultures circled in the air. Some Hindus came out of the temple, where they had brought flowers to the

Buddha. The gentle depth of their eyes, the nobility of their brows, the suffering fragility of their bodies, consumed by fever, the biblical slowness of their gait—all that moved me to the depths of my being. They seemed in exile on their native soil, close to their kindly God, chained and watched over by Sepoys. And there was no longer anything earthly in their black pupils... nothing more than a dream of corporeal release, awaiting the dazzling light of nirvana. I do not know what feeling of respect for humanity prevented me from kneeling before these sorrowful, venerable fathers of my race—my parricidal race. I merely saluted them humbly, but they passed by without seeing me—without seeing my greeting—without seeing the tears in my eyes and the filial emotion which swelled my breast. And when they had passed by I felt that I hated Europe with a hatred that would never be extinguished." Suddenly interrupting herself, she said:

"But I'm boring you, eh? I don't know why I'm telling you all this. It has no bearing on the subject. I'm crazy!"

"No, no, dear Clara," I replied, kissing her hands. "To the contrary, I love you to talk to me like that. Always talk to me like that!" She continued:

"After visiting the poor bare little temple, whose entrance was decorated by a gong—the only vestige of its former wealth—after breathing the odor of the flowers with which the image of the Buddha was all strewn, I went sadly back to the city. It was deserted. That grotesque and sinister manifestation of Occidental progress, a pastor—the only human being—was prowling about, skirting the walls, a lotus blossom stuck in his mouth. In that blinding sunlight he had preserved—as in the city fogs—his ridiculous clergyman's costume; a soft black felt hat, a long black coat with a tight, greasy collar, and black trousers falling in ugly folds over the massive boots of a drayman. This dingy costume of a Protestant preacher was accompanied by a white parasol, a sort of ridiculous, portable *punka,* the sole concession the bigot made to the local customs and the Indian sun which the English have not to this day been able to turn into a sooty fog. And I irritably reflected that you can't take a step from the equator to the poles without running into that suspicious face, those rapacious eyes, those claw like hands and that vile mouth, which goes breathing the frightful verses of the Bible, in an odor of stale gin, over the charming divinities and adorable myths of naive religions."

She grew excited. Her eyes expressed an overwhelming hatred which I would never have expected of them. Forgetting where we were, and her recent criminal enthusiasms and bloody exaltations, she said:

"Wherever there is spilt blood to justify, piracy to consecrate, violation to bless, hideous traffic to protect, you are sure to see this British Tartuffe pursuing the work of abominable conquest under the pretext of religious proselytism or scientific study. His cruel and crafty shadow is cast over the wreckage of conquered people, coupled with that of the cutthroat soldier and the usurious Shylock. In the virgin forests where the European is more rightfully feared than the tiger, on the threshold of the humble, devastated hut, between the burning cabins, he appears after the massacre like the hangers-on of an army come to rifle the dead in the evening of a battle. A crony worthy of his rival, the Catholic missionary, who also brings civilization at the flame of a torch, and the point of a saber or a bayonet. Alas, China is invaded and devoured by these two scourges! In a few years nothing will remain of this marvelous country where I love so much to live!" Suddenly she got up, uttering a cry:

"And the bell, my love! I can't hear the bell any more. Ah, my God, he'll be dead! While we were here, talking, they probably took him to the morgue, and we won't see him! It's your fault too... " She made me get up from the bench.

"Quick, quick, darling!"

"We're not in a hurry, my dear Clara. We'll always see enough horrors. Speak to me some more as you Were speaking a moment ago, when I loved your voice so much; when I loved your eyes so much!" She grew impatient:

"Quick, quick! You don't know what you're saying!" Her eyes had become hard again, her voice panting, her mouth imperiously cruel and sensual. Then it seemed to me that the Buddha's face itself, distorted by the sunlight, became the twisted, sneering face of an executioner. And I saw the young girl who had made her offering, going away down a path between the lawns, in the distance. Her yellow dress was very small, light and gleaming, like a narcissus blossom.

The path we walked on was bordered by peach trees, cherry trees, wild quince and almond trees, some dwarfed and trimmed in bizarre shapes, others free, bushy, and thrusting their long branches laden with flowers in every direction. A little apple tree, whose wood, leaves, and blossoms were bright red, assumed the form of a bulging vase. I also noticed an admirable tree, which is called the birch-leaf pear tree. It rose in a perfect pyramid to a height of six meters, and from its wide base to its sharp cone-shaped tip, it was so covered with flowers that neither its leaves nor branches were visible. Innumerable petals continuously dropped off and others opened, and they fluttered around the pyramid and floated slowly onto the paths and lawns, covering them with the whiteness of snow. And the air in the distance was impregnated with the subtle scents of egrantine and mignonette. Then we skirted clumps of shrubbery decorated with tiny-flowered deutzias in large pink clusters, and those pretty Pekin ligustrums with their shaggy foliage and great feathery panicles of white flowers powdered with sulphur.

At every step there was a fresh delight and a surprise for the eyes, which made me utter cries of admiration. Here there was a vine, whose broad light leaves I had noticed in the mountains of Annam, irregularly indented and denticulated—as denticulated and indented and broad as castor-oil leaves, which enlaced an immense dead tree with its tendrils, climbed to the topmost branches and from there fell in a cascade, a cataract, an avalanche, sheltering from the sun an entire flora, which blossomed out at the base between the leaves, colonnades amid niches formed by its tumbling twigs. There, a stephanotis displayed its paradoxical foliage, preciously wrought like cloisonne, and I marveled at its multiple gradations of color, from peacock-green to steel-blue, from a delicate pink to a barbaric purple, and from a light yellow to a rich brown ochre. Close by, a group of gigantic viburnums, as high as oaks, shook snowy globes at the tip of every branch.

From place to place gardeners, kneeling in the grass or perched on red ladders, were training clematis over fine bamboo armatures; others were twining ipomcea and calystegia about long thin props of black wood. And everywhere on the lawns, lilies lifted their stalks ready to blossom.

Trees, bushes, clumps of foliage, isolated or clustered plants, seemed at first to have grown wherever their seed had fallen at random, uncared for, without any other will than nature's, without any other design than that of life itself. It was an error. To the contrary, the location of every plant had been laboriously studied and chosen, either so the colors and forms would complement each other and set each other off, or so as not to interfere with plans, aerial perspectives and floral vistas, and thus multiply sensations by combining patterns. The humblest flower as well as the greatest tree assisted in an unbroken harmony by its very position,' in an ensemble of art whose effect was all the more stirring by the very fact that it gave no appearance of geometrical labor or decorative effort.

Everything seemed also to have been arranged by the munificence of nature, for the triumph of peonies.

On the gentle slopes, sown like lawns, lay strips of odorous woodruff and pink crucianella, roses the color known as old rose, and fields of arborescent peonies like sumptuous carpets. Near by there were single blossoms that held out to us their immense calyxes, red, black, copper, orange, and purple. Others, ideally pure, offered the most virginal shades of pink and white. The peonies were actual fairies, miraculous queens of this miraculous garden. They were gathered in glistening masses, or lay singly beside the path, meditative at the foot of the trees and amorous beside the clumps of shrubbery.

Wherever the eye wandered, it encountered a peony. On the stone bridges, entirely covered with saxatile plants, whose bold sweep bound the masses of rock together and lay on paths between the kiosks, peonies marched by like a holiday throng. Their brilliant procession scaled the hillocks around which the alleys and paths, bordered by slender silver prickwood and privet trimmed in hedges, climbed, crossed and tangled. I admired a little knoll where, protected by mats on very low, white walls built like snail-shells, there stretched the most precious species of peonies, warped by clever artists onto an intricate lattice. In the gaps between these walls, perennial peonies bunched on high, bare stems, were spaced in square boxes. And the summit was crowned with thick clusters and massy bushes of the sacred plant which blossoms so rarely in Europe, but flourishes here throughout the year. And at my right, at my left, near by or quite lost in the distance, there lay forever and ever, peonies, peonies, and peonies...

Clara had started to walk very rapidly again, almost insensible to all this beauty; she walked, her forehead barred by a hard shadow, her pupils glowing. She seemed carried away by some destructive power. She spoke, and I heard nothing—or very little, of what she said. The words, 'death', 'charm', 'torture', and 'love', which fell ceaselessly from her lips, seemed no more to me than a distant echo, the tiny voice of a scarcely audible bell far, far off, and melting into the glory, triumphs, and serene and stupendous passion of this dazzling life about me.

Clara walked and walked, and I walked beside her, and everywhere there was a fresh surprise: peonies, dreamlike or fantastic bushes, blue prickwood, violently streaked holly, plaited and twisting magnolias, dwarf cedars which were ruffled like a head of hair, aralia and tall grass, giant eulalia, whose ribbon-like leaves hung and swayed like snake-skins flaked with gold. There were also tropical species; unknown trees on whose trunks obscene orchids swayed; the Indian banyan, rooted in the soil by its multiple branches; immense nusas, and in the shade of their leaves, flowers like insects, like birds, such as the fairylike strelitzia, whose yellow petals are wings and flutter ceaselessly.

Suddenly Clara halted as though an invisible hand had brutally been laid upon her. Anxious, tense, her nostrils palpitating like a doe's which has just scented the odor of the male on the wind, she inhaled the air about her. A shiver, which I recognized as the forerunner of a spasm, ran through her entire body. Her lips instantly became red and swollen.

"Did you smell it?" she said, in an abrupt, hollow voice.

"I smell the aroma of the peonies which fills the garden," I replied. She stamped on the earth with an impatient foot:

"It's not that! Didn't you smell it? Try to remember!" And, her nostrils dilating, her eyes more brilliant, she said:

"It smells like when I love you!"

Then quickly, she bent over a plant, a thalictrum which lifted a long, branching, light violet stem beside the path. Each auxiliary branch issued from an ivory-like sheath the shape of a yoni, and ended in a cluster of tiny little flowers, thickly bunched and covered with pollen:

"This is it! This is it! Oh my darling!"

In fact, a powerful phosphoric odor, an odor of semen rose from this plant. Clara plucked its stalk, forced me to breathe the strange odor; then, sprinkling my face with pollen:

"Oh, darling! darling!" she said, "what a lovely plant! How it intoxicates me. How it maddens me! Is it strange that there are plants that smell of love? Why not? You don't know? Well, I do! Why are there so many flowers like human organs, if not because nature ceaselessly cries to living beings in all her forms, and all her perfumes: 'Love each other! love each other! Be like the flowers. There is nothing but love!' Oh, tell me quickly, darling little swine... " She continued to inhale the odor of the thalictrum and chewed at the cluster, whose pollen stuck to her lips. And abruptly she declared:

"I want them in my garden... I want them in my room... in the kiosk... in all the house. Smell, darling, smell! A simple plant, isn't it wonderful! And now, come... come! If only we don't get there too late... to the bell!" With a pout, which was both comical and tragic, she continued:

"Why did you linger down there on that bench? Don't look at all these flowers; don't look at them anymore! You'll see them better later—after seeing suffering and death. You'll see how much more beautiful they are, and what ardent passion their perfumes excite! Smell again, darling; and come! And feel my breasts. How firm they are! The silk of my dress excites their nipples... it feels like a hot iron burning them. It's delicious. Come now!"

She started to run, her face all yellow with pollen, and the stalk of the thalictrum between her teeth.

Clara did not care to halt before another image of Buddha, whose face, wrinkled and devoured by time, grimaced in the sunlight. A woman was offering it cydonia branches, and these flowers seemed like little children's hearts to me. At the turn of the alley, we passed a litter carried by two men, on which there stirred a bundle of bleeding flesh; a sort of human being, whose skin, cut in strips, trailed on the ground like rags. Although it was impossible to recognize the slightest vestige of humanity in that hideous wound which, moreover, once had been a man. I felt that by some miracle it was still breathing. And drops of blood spotted the pathway.

Clara plucked two peonies and laid them silently upon the litter with a trembling hand. With a brutal smile, the porters bared their black gums and their lacquered teeth, and when the litter had passed:

"Ah, ah! I see the bell," said Clara, "I see the bell!" And all about us, and all about the litter disappearing in the distance, there was like a rosy, white, and mauve rain, a variegated shimmering, a pearly, pink, and milky pulsation so tender and changing that it is impossible for me to express in words its infinite sweetness and ineffable idyllic poetry...

PART 6

We left the curving alley into which other alleys branch on their circuitous way to the center, and which runs along an embankment planted with many rare and precious, shrubs, and took a little path which follows a dip in the land and ends directly at the bell. Paths and alleys were sanded with pulverized brick, which gave to the green of the lawns and foliage an extraordinary intensity and the transparence of an emerald under the light of a chandelier. To the right there were flowering lawns; to the left, more shrubbery. Pink acers rubbed with pale silver, bright gold, bronze or red—copper; mahonia, whose leaves of reddish-brown copper were broad as the leaves of a cocoanut palm; eleagnus, which seemed to have been coated with polychrome lacquer; pyrus, powdered with mica; laurel, on which there twinkled and glittered the thousand facets of a variegated crystal; caladium, whose veins of old gold set off the embroidered silks and Pink lace of the blossom; arbor vitre both blue, mauve, silver and plumed with sickly yellows and poisonous orange; pale tamarisk, green tamarisk, red tamarisk, whose branches swayed and floated in the air like slender alga: in the sea; cotton-plants, whose tufts took flight and traveled ceaselessly through the air; salix and its joyous swarm of winged seeds; and clerodendron, spreading its large scarlet bells like parasols. In the sunny spaces between these shrubs, anemones, ranunculus and heucliera were sprinkled through the grass; in the shady spots strange cryptograms showed themselves, mosses covered with minute white flowerlets, and lichens like agglomerations of polyps and clumps of madrepores. It was a perpetual enchantment.

And in the midst of this floral magic, there arose scaffolds, the apparatus of crucifixion, gibbets with violent decorations and black gallows, on whose tops there leered frightful demon masks; high gallows for simple strangulation, lower gibbets mechanically equipped for the tearing of flesh. On the shafts of these torture columns—as a diabolic refinement—pubescent calystegia, ipomcea from Daoura, lophospermum and colocynth spread their blossoms, and clematis and atragene. Birds piped their love-songs there.

At the foot of one of these gibbets, covered with flowers like the column of a terrace, an executioner was seated, his instrument-case between his feet, cleaning his fine steel implements with silk cloths; his gown was all covered with splattered blood and his hands seemed gloved in red. Around him, as around a corpse, there hummed and whirled swarms of flies. But in this haven of flowers and perfumes, this was neither repugnant nor terrible—it seemed that petals from a neighboring quince tree had rained upon his robe. Besides, he had a peaceful and good-natured belly. His face, in repose, expressed kindliness and even joviality; the joviality of a surgeon who has just brought a difficult operation to a successful finish. As we passed, he lifted his eyes and greeted us politely. Clara spoke to him in English.

"It's really too bad you didn't come along an hour earlier," this good man said, "you'd have seen something very lovely... something that isn't seen every day. An extraordinary job, milady. I rebuilt a man from head to foot, after removing his entire skin. He was so badly built! Ha! ha!"

Trembling with laughter, his belly alternately swelled and sank with a hollow, rumbling sound. A nervous tic lifted the slit of his mouth up to his cheekbone and, at the same time, his lowered eyelids touched the edge of his lips, amid the fat folds of his face. And this grimace, which was a multitude of grimaces, gave his face an expression of comical and macabre cruelty. Clara asked:

"Doubtless he's the one we met just now on the litter?"

"Ah, you met him?" exclaimed the good man, flattered. "Well, what did you think of him?"

"How horrible!" said Clara, in a tranquil voice which belied her exclamation of disgust. Then the executioner explained:

"Be was a miserable harbor coolie... nothing at all, milady. He really didn't deserve the honor of so fine a piece of work. It seems he stole a sack of rice from the English... our dear, good friends, the English. When I had taken off his skin, and it hung to his shoulders only by two little buttons, I made him walk, milady! ha! ha! Truly, a great idea! You'd have split your sides. He seemed to be wearing—what do you call the thing?—ah, yes, indeed! an inverness? Never had the dog been better dressed, nor by a better tailor. But he had bones so hard I chipped my saw on them—this beautiful saw."

A little, whitish, greasy bit remained between the teeth of the saw. With a flip of the nail he made it leap and sent it off into the grass, among the flowerlets.

"That's marrow, milady," said the jolly old fellow. "He didn't have too much of it." And shaking his head, he added: "They very seldom have much of it, for we work almost exclusively with the lower class." Then, with an air of tranquil satisfaction:

"Yesterday, it was very strange. I made a woman out of a man. He! he! And it was such a good job you couldn't tell the difference, and I myself was fooled looking at him. Tomorrow, if the genii grant me a woman on this gibbet, I'll make a man of her. That's not as easy! Ha, ha!"

Under the stimulus of another laugh, his triple chin, the pads of his neck, and his belly trembled like jelly. A single, red, arched line then joined the left corner of his mouth to the seam of his left eyelid, among the puffs and furrows from which flowed little streams of sweat and tears of laughter.

He put the cleansed and gleaming saw into the case and closed it. Its box was lovely and of an excellent lacquer: a flight of wild geese over a nocturnal pool, where the moon silvered the lotus and the iris. At that moment, the shadow of the gallows threw a transverse purple bar across the body of the executioner.

"You see, milady," continued the talkative fellow, "our trade, just like our lovely vases, our beautiful embroidered silks, and lovely lacquers, is disappearing little by little. Today we no longer know what torture really is, although I try to carryon its real tradition. I am swamped, and I can't stay its decadence all by myself. What can you do? Now they recruit executioners from God knows where! No more examinations, no more competitions. Influence and protection alone decide their choice. And what choices, if you only knew! It's shameful! In the olden days, they only entrusted these important functions to actual scientists, men of merit who knew the anatomy of the human body perfectly, who had diplomas, experience, or natural talent. Today what the hell! The merest shoemaker can presume to fill these honorable and difficult positions. No more hierarchy,. no more traditions! Everything is disappearing, for we live in a chaotic age. There is something rotten in China, milady." He sighed deeply, and showing us his red hands, and the instrument case gleaming in the grass beside him, he continued his long recital:

"However, I do the best I can, as you have seen, to resurrect our abolished prestige. For I'm an old conservative myself, an uncompromising nationalist, and I despise all these practices, all these new methods which the Europeans, and particularly the English, are bringing us under pretext of civilization. I should not care to slander the English, milady; they are honest and very respectable people. But you must admit their influence on our customs has been disastrous. Every day they deprive our China of its unique character. From the point of view of torture alone, milady, they have done us much harm... much harm. It's a great shame!"

"They know how, however," Clara interrupted, wounded in her national pride by this reproach; for though she really desired to display severity towards her compatriots, whom she detested, she intended to have them respected by all others.

The executioner shrugged his shoulders and, compelled by his nervous tic, succeeded in displaying the most provocatively comical grimace that could ever be seen upon a human face. And while, despite our horror, we had great difficulty in suppressing our laughter, he declared peremptorily:

"No, milady, they don't know how at all! In this matter, they are actual savages. Look—in India—let's consider India alone—what a vulgar, inartistic business! And how stupidly—yes, stupidly—they've wasted death!" He clasped his bloody hands as in prayer, lifted his eyes to heaven, and in a lugubrious voice which seemed to ring with tears of regret he went on to say:

"When you think, milady," he exclaimed, "of all the wonderful things they might have done down there... and which they haven't done... and which they'll never do! It's unpardonable!"

"There, for instance," Clara protested, "you don't know what you're talking about."

"May the genii carry me off if I lie!" exclaimed the fat old fellow. And in a slower voice, with didactic gestures, he stated:

"In torture, as in everything, the English are not artists; All the admirable qualities you wish, milady, but not that... no, no, no!"

"Come now! they've made the whole world weep!"

"Bad, milady... very bad," corrected the executioner. "Art does not consist in killing multitudes... in slaughtering, massacring, and exterminating men in hordes. Really, it's too easy. Art, milady, consists in knowing how to kill, according to the rites of beauty, whose divine secret we Chinese alone possess. Know how to kill! Nothing is rarer, and everything depends on that. Know how to kill! That is to say, how to work the human body like a sculptor works his day or piece of ivory, and evoke the entire sum, every prodigy of suffering it conceals in the depths of its shadows and its mysteries. There! Science is required, variety, taste, imagination... genius, after all. But today, everything is disappearing. The Occidental snobbery which is invading us, the gunboats, rapid-fire guns, long-range rifles, explosives... what else? Everything which makes death collective, administrative and bureaucratic—all the filth of your progress, in fact—is destroying, little by little, our beautiful traditions of the past. It is only here, in this garden, that they are conserved as well as can be... where we try at least to maintain them as well as possible. But what difficulties! what obstacles! what continual struggles—if you knew! Alas, I feel it won't last much longer. We have been conquered by mediocrity, and the bourgeois spirit is triumphing everywhere—"

His face then possessed a singular expression of both melancholy and pride, while his gestures revealed profound lassitude.

"And besides," he said. "I who speak to you, milady—I'm certainly not just anybody. I can boast of having disinterestedly worked all my life to the glory of our great Empire. I have always been first in the competitive examinations in torture—and in many of them. I have invented—believe me—things actually sublime, wonderful tortures which, in another time and under another dynasty, would have made my fortune and spelled immortality. Well, they scarcely pay any attention to me. I'm not understood. Let us say the word: they despise me. What can you expect? Today talent counts for nothing; it isn't given the slightest recognition. It's discouraging, I assure you! Poor China, once so artistic, so magnificently celebrated! Ah, I really fear it's ripe for conquest!" With a pessimistic and broken-hearted-gesture, he took Clara to witness to this decadence, and his grimaces were utterly untranslatable.

"After all—look milady! Isn't it lamentable? I'm the man who invented the torture of the rat. May the genii devour my liver if it wasn't I! Ah, milady, an extraordinary torture, I swear. Originality, picturesqueness, psychology, the science of pain—it had everything in its favor. And the bargain, it was infinitely comical. It was inspired by that ancient Chinese gaiety, so neglected in our day. Ah, how it would have excited everyone's good spirits. What a resource for languishing conversations! Well, they've renounced it. Worse, they'd have nothing to do with it. And yet, the three trials we held before the judges met with such a colossal success."

As we did not seem to pity him, and these recriminations of an old employee rather annoyed us, the executioner repeated, emphasizing the word:

"Colossal... co-los-sal!"

"What is this torture of the rat," Clara asked, "and how does it happen that I don't know about it?"

"A masterpiece, milady—a perfect masterpiece!" the fat man insisted in a resounding voice, and his flabby body settled more and more into the grass.

"I heard you... and then?"

"A masterpiece, in truth! And you see... you don't know about it... nobody knows anything about it. What a pity! How can you expect me not to be humiliated?"

"Can you describe it to us?"

"Can I! I absolutely can. I'm going to explain it to you, and you'll judge. Follow me carefully... " And the fat man, sketching shapes in the air with precise gestures, spoke as follows:

"You take a condemned man, charming lady, a condemned man, or anybody else—for it isn't necessary for the success of my torture that the victim be condemned to anything at all—you take a man, as young and strong as possible, whose muscles are quite resistant; in virtue of this principle: the more strength, the more struggle and the more struggle, the more pain! Good. You undress him. Good. And when he is stark naked—yes, milady?—you make him kneel, his back bent, on the earth, where you fasten him with chains riveted to iron collars which bind his neck, his wrists, his calves and ankles. Good! I don't know whether I'm making myself understood? Then in a big pot, whose bottom is pierced with a little hole—a flowerpot, milady!—you place a very fat rat, whom it's wise to have deprived of nourishment for a couple of days, to excite its ferocity. And this pot, inhabited by this rat, you apply hermetically, like an enormous cupping-glass, to the back of the condemned by means of stout thongs attached to a leather girdle about the loins. Ah, hat Now the plot thickens!"

He looked maliciously at us out of the corners of his lowered lids, to judge the effect his words were producing.

"And then?" said Clara, simply.

"Then, milady, you introduce into the little hole into the pot—guess what!"

"How should l know?"

The good fellow rubbed his hands, smiled horribly, and then continued:

"You introduce an iron rod, heated red-hot at the fire of a forge—a little portable forge which is there beside you. And when the iron rod is introduced, what happens? Ah, ha hat Imagine what must happen, milady—"

"Oh, come on, you old gossip!" commanded my companion, and stamped angrily on the sandy path.

"There, there!" said the prolix executioner. "A little patience, milady. And let us proceed methodically, if you please. Well, you introduce into the pot's hole, an iron rod, heated red-hot at the fire of a forge. The rat tries to escape the burning of the rod and its dazzling light. It goes mad, cuts capers, leaps and bounds, runs around the walls of the pot, crawls and gallops over the roan's flesh, which it first tickles and then tears with its nails, and bites with its sharp teeth, seeking an exit through the torn and bleeding skin. But there is no exit. During the first frenzied moments, the rat can find none. And the iron rod, handled cleverly and slowly, still draws near the rat, threatens it, scorches its fur. What do you think of this for a beginning?" He caught his breath for a few seconds, then staidly, authoritatively, he instructed us:

"It's great merit lies in the fact that you must know how to prolong this initial operation as much as possible, for the laws of physiology teach us that there is nothing more horrible to the human flesh than the combination of tickling and biting. It may even happen that the victim goes mad from it. He howls and struggles; his body, remaining free between the iron collars, palpitates, heaves and contorts, shaken by agonizing shudders. But his limbs are firmly held by the chains, and the pot, by the thongs. And the movements of the condemned man only augment the rat's fury, to which the intoxication of blood is often added. It's sublime, milady!"

"And then?" said Clara, grown slightly pale, in an abrupt, unsteady voice.

The executioner clacked his tongue, and continued:

"Finally—for I see you're anxious to know the climax of this wonderful and jolly story; finally threatened by the glowing rod and thanks to the excitation of a few well-chosen burns, the rat ends by finding an exit, milady. Ah, ha ha!"

"How horrible!" exclaimed Clara.

"Ah, you see... I'm proud of the interest you take in my torture. But wait! The rat penetrates the man's body, widening with claws and teeth the opening he madly digs, as in the earth. And he croaks, stifled, at the same time that the victim who, after a half-hour of ineffable, incomparable torture, ends by succumbing to a hemorrhage—when it isn't from too much suffering or even the congestion caused by a frightful insanity. In all cases, milady, and whatever the final cause of this death—you can be sure it's extremely beautiful!"

Satisfied, and with an air of triumphant pride, he concluded:

"Isn't it extremely beautiful, milady? Isn't it actually a prodigious invention? an admirable masterpiece, classic after a fashion, and whose equivalent you may vainly seek in the past? I would not like to be lacking in modesty, milady, but agree that the demons who used to haunt the forests of Yunnam never conceived a like miracle. Well, the judges would have nothing to do with it! There I brought them, you'll admit, something infinitely glorious, something unique in its fashion, capable of inspiring our greatest artists. They didn't want it... they want nothing... nothing at all! The return to the classic tradition terrifies them. Without also counting all sorts of moral obstacles, painful to relate... intrigue, extortion, underhand rivalry, scorn of equity, horror of the beautiful—and what not? you'd have thought, at least, I'm sure, that for such a service they'd have made me a mandarin. Indeed! Nothing, milady—I received nothing! There are the symptoms characteristic of our downfall. Ah, we are a lost people, a dead people! Let the Japanese come; we can no longer resist them. Farewell China!"

He was silent. The sun, sinking in the west, the shadow of the gallows then shifted with the sun, and lay stretched across the grass. The lawns became a brighter green; a sort of pink and gold mist rose from the watered bushes, and the flowers shone more brilliantly, like little variegated stars in the firmament of foliage. A yellow bird carrying a long cotton-twig in its beak, repaired its nest in the depths of the leafage which covered the shaft of the torture column at whose foot the executioner was seated. Now he was dreaming, with a more placid countenance and less violent grimaces, in which cruelty was replaced by melancholy.

"Just like the flowers," he murmured, after a silence. A black cat which had emerged from the bushes, its back arched and its tail hanging, came and rubbed itself against him, purring. He caressed it gently. Then, having noticed a scarabee, the cat stretched out behind a tuft of grass and, its ears erect, its eyes glowing, started to follow the capricious flight of the insect in the air. The executioner, whose patriotic lamentations had been interrupted by the cat, shook his head and continued:

"Just like the flowers! We have also lost the sense of flowers, for one thing follows another. We no longer know what flowers are. Would you believe that they are sending us some from Europe—we who possess the most varied and extraordinary flora on the globe. What aren't they sending us today? Helmets, bicycles, furniture, coffee-mills, wine and flowers! And if you knew the sad stupidities, the sentimental nonsense and decadent follies our poets utter on the subject of flowers. It's frightful! There are some who assert they are perverse! Flowers perverse! In fact, they no longer know what to write. Have you ever heard such monstrous nonsense, milady? Why, flowers are violent, cruel, terrible and splendid... like love!"

He picked a ranunculus which gently swayed its golden head above the grass beside him, and with infinite delicacy, slowly and amorously, he turned it between his fat red fingers, from which the dried blood scaled off in places:

"Isn't it adorable?" he repeated, looking at it. "It's so little, so fragile, and besides, it's all of nature; all the beauty and power of nature. It contains the world. A puny and relentless organism which goes straight to the goal of its desire! Ah, milady, flowers do not indulge in sentiment. They indulge in passion, nothing but passion. And they make love all the time, and in every fashion. They think of nothing else; and how right they are! Perverse? Because they obey the only law of life; because they are satisfied with the only need of life, which is love? But consider, milady, the flower is only a reproductive organ. Is there anything healthier, stronger, or more beautiful than that? These marvelous petals, these silks, these velvets... these soft, supple, and caressing materials are the curtains of the alcove, the draperies of the bridal chamber, the perfumed bed where they unite, where they pass their ephemeral and immortal life, swooning with love. What an admirable example for us!"

He spread the petals of the flower, counted the stamens laden with pollen, and he spoke again, his eyes swimming in a comical ecstasy:

"See, milady; one, two, five, ten, twenty. See how they quiver! Look! Sometimes twenty males are required for the delight of a single female! He! he! he! Sometimes it's the opposite." One by one he tore off the petals of the flower:

"And when they are gorged with love, then the curtains of the bed are torn away, the draperies of the chamber wither and fall; and the flowers die, because they know well they have nothing more to do. They die, to be reborn later, and once again, to love!" Throwing the stripped peduncle away, he exclaimed:

"Make love, milady... make love... like the flowers!"

Then abruptly he took up his instrument-case, got up, his queue awry, and saluting us, went away across the lawn, treading with his heavy, swaying body upon the grass blossoming with squill, doronicum and narcissus. For some moments Clara followed him with her eyes, and as we started to walk towards the bell:

"Isn't he funny! What a roly-poly!" she said. "He's so good natured." I stupidly exclaimed in my horror:

"How can you say such a thing, my dear Clara? Why, he's a monster! It's even frightful to think such a monster exists among men, somewhere in the world! I feel that from now on I'll always have the nightmare of that horrible face before me, and the horror of that conversation. You hurt me very much, I assure you." Clara replied quickly:

"And you hurt me too. Why do you pretend the roly-poly is a monster? You don't know anything about it. He loves his art, that's all; like a sculptor loves sculpture, and like a musician loves music. And he talks about it marvelously! It's curious and aggravating that you refuse to get it into your head we are in China, and not, thank God, in Hyde Park or the Bodiniere, among all those dirty bourgeois you adore! As far as you're concerned, the customs of all countries should be identical—and what customs! A lovely idea! Don't you realize it would mean dying of monotony, and the end of travel, my dear!" Then suddenly, in a more decided tone of reproach:

"Ah, really, you're not at all nice. Your egoism never relaxes for a second, not even when I request the slightest pleasure of you. It's impossible to even enjoy oneself a little with you; you're never happy with anything. Without counting the fact that thanks to you, we've probably missed the best!" She sighed sadly:

"Here's another day lost! I have no luck." I tried to justify myself and calm her:

"No... no," insisted Clara, "it's very bad. You're not a man. Even when Annie was alive, it was the same thing. You spoiled all our pleasure—fainting like a little boarding-school girl or a pregnant woman. People like you stay at home. God, how stupid. We go out gaily, happily, to have a good-time, see sublime sights, be thrilled by extraordinary sensations... and then suddenly you're sad, and it's all over! No, no! It's stupid, stupid... it's too stupid!" She hung more heavily on my arm, and she pouted—a pout of annoyance and affection—so exquisite I felt a thrill of desire run through my veins.

"And I who do everything you want, like a poor puppy," she moaned. Then:

"I'm sure you think me wicked, because I enjoy things that make you grow pale and tremble. You think me wicked and heartless, don't you?" Without waiting for a reply, she confessed:

"But I grow pale too, and I also tremble. Otherwise I wouldn't enjoy myself. Well, do you think me wicked?"

"No, dear Clara, you are not wicked... you are—" She quickly interrupted me, offered her lips to me:

"I'm not wicked. I don't want you to think me wicked. I'm a nice little woman... curious, like all women. And you, you're only an old hen! I don't love you any more. Kiss your mama, darling. Kiss hard... harder... harder. No, I don't love you any more—like milksop. Yes, by God, that's it... you're only a darling little insignificant milksop."

Gay, yet serious, smiling, but her forehead barred by the dark fold of shadow she possessed in anger as well as passion, she added:

"Say I'm only a woman... a very little woman... a woman as fragile as a flower... as delicate and frail as a bamboo-stalk... and that of the two of us, I'm the man... and that I'm worth ten men like you!"

And the desire her flesh provoked in me was augmented by an immense pity for her mad, lost soul. Once more, with a slight hiss of scorn, she said that phrase, which came so often to her lips:

"Men! They don't know what love is, nor what death is, which is much more beautiful than love. They don't know anything, and they're always sad, and weep! And faint for no reason, Over nothings! Phht! phht! phht!" Changing her line of thought, like a beetle shifting from one flower to the next, she suddenly asked:

"Is it true what that roly-poly just told us?"

"What, dear Clara? And ,what difference does he make to you?"

"Just now the roly-poly said that among the flowers, twenty males were sometimes required for the delight of a single female. Is it true?"

"Certainly!"

"Really true? Really... really true?"

"Obviously."

"The roly-poly wasn't making fun of us? Are you sure?" "You're funny! Why do you ask that? Why do you look at me with such strange eyes? Of course it's true."

"Ah!"

She remained pensive, her lids closed for a moment. Her breath came hurriedly, her breast almost panted. Then, very low, she murmured, resting her head against my chest:

"I'd like to be a flower. I'd like... I'd like to be—everything!"

"Clara!" I begged, "my little Clara." I held her fast in my arms. I cradled her in my arms.

"Wouldn't you? You wouldn't like to? Oh—you'd rather stay a little milksop all your life! Pugh, how naughty!" After a short silence, during which we even heard the red sand of the alley crunch beneath our heavy steps, she continued, in a singing voice:

"And I'd also like... when I am dead... I'd like to have very strong perfumes put in my coffin... thalictrum blossoms... and images of sin... beautiful, exciting, naked images, like those that decorate the mats in my room. Or better, I'd like to be buried without a dress or a shroud, in the crypts of the temple of Elephanta, amid all those strange stone bacchantes, who caress and tear each other so furiously. Ah, my darling! I'd like... I'd like to be dead already!" And abruptly:

"When you're dead, do your feet touch the wood of the coffin?"

"Clara!" I implored. "Why are you always talking of death? And still you don't want me to be sad! I beg you, don't drive me completely mad. Give up these sordid ideas that torment me so and let's go home. For pity's sake, dear Clara, let's go home."

She did not listen to my plea, and continued in a musical tone which I couldn't tell... no, truthfully, I could not tell whether it expressed emotion or irony, convulsive sobs or hysterical laughter.

"If you are with me when I die... darling... listen to me! Please put... yes, that's the thing... please put a pretty little yellow silk cushion between my poor little feet and the wood of the casket. And then, please kill my handsome Laos hound... and stretch him out, still bleeding, beside me... like he himself is accustomed to stretch out, you know, with one paw on my thigh and another on my breast. And then... for a long, long time, please kiss me darling, on my teeth... and my hair. And tell me things... pretty things... things that soothe and excite... things like when you love me. Won't you, my darling? Promise me? Come now, don't make such a funereal face. It isn't dying that's sad; it's living when you're not happy. Swear! Swear that you promise me!"

"Clara! Clara! I beg you! Be quiet!"

I was undoubtedly at the end of my strength. A flood of tears gushed from my eyes. I wouldn't have been able to tell the reason for these tears, which were not tears of distress, and which, to the contrary, gave me relief and relaxation. And Clara was deceived in attributing them to herself. It wasn't for her I was weeping, nor for her sin, nor for the pity which her poor, sick soul inspired in me, nor for the image of her death she had just evoked. It was for myself I was weeping, perhaps, for my presence in this garden, for this cursed love in which I felt that everything which then remained to me every generous impulse, every lost desire, and every noble ambition was profaned by the impure breath of these kisses, of which I was ashamed and for which I was also thirsty. Well, no! Why should I lie to myself? physical tears... tears of weakness, fatigue and fever, tears of enervation before sights too cruel for my debilitated senses, before odors too strong for my sense of smell, before the continual oscillation of my carnal desires from impotence to frenzy... the tears of a woman... tears for nothing at all!

Certain that it was because of her, because of her dead... because of her stretched out in her coffin I was weeping, and happy in her power over me, Clara became deliciously cajoling:

"Poor little pet!" she sighed. "You're trying! Well then, say the roly-poly was good-natured. Say it to please me and I'll be quiet, and never talk of death again... never again. Come, right now, say it, little pig."

In a cowardly fashion, but also anxious to be finished at last with all these macabre ideas, I did what she asked. With clamorous joy, she fell on my neck, kissed me on the lips, and drying my eyes, exclaimed:

"Ah, you're nice! You're a nice baby! A darling little baby, my darling! And I'm a vile woman, a wicked little woman who's always teasing you and making you cry. Well then, the roly-poly is a monster... I detest him. And I don't want you to kill my beautiful Laos hound. And I don't want to die. And I adore you, ah! And then... and then... all this is just to make you laugh, you understand. Don't cry any more, ah, don't cry any more! Now smile! Smile with your lovely eyes, with your mouth which can say such tender things... your mouth, your mouth! And let's walk faster. I love so much to walk very fast, on your arm!"

And head to head we walked, her parasol above us fluttering lightly, brilliantly, and madly, like an enormous butterfly.

PART 7

We were approaching the bell. On the right and left there were immense red and purple flowers and blood-colored peonies, and in the shade, under enormous parasol-shaped leaves, petasites and anthuriums like bleeding tissues seemed ironically to greet us on the way, and point out the path of torture to us. There were other flowers also, flowers of butchery and massacre, tiger-flowers with their gaping mutilated throats, diclytras and their garlands of little red hearts, and fierce labiates with their firm and fleshy pulp the tint of mucus; they were veritable human lips—Clara's lips crying from the tops of their tender stalks:

"Come, my dears, come quickly. Where you are going there is still more pain, more torture, more blood flowing and dripping on the earth, more contorted and torn bodies breathing their last on iron tables... more ragged flesh swaying on the gallows-rope, more horror and more hell. Come, my loves, come, lip to lip and hand in hand. And look between the foliage and the lattice-work, look at the infernal diorama unfolding, and the diabolic festival of death!"

Clara was silent, shivering, her teeth clenched, her eyes more glowing and cruel. She was silent and walked, listening to these flower-voices in which she recognized her own, that voice of frightful days and homicidal nights, the voice of cruelty and lust, and also pain, which seemed to come not only from the depths of the earth and the abyss of death, but at the same time from the deeper and blacker depths of her own soul.

A strident noise like the creaking of a pulley filled the air. Then there was another sound, very sweet, very pure, like the resonance of a crystal cup which a moth had struck in its evening flight. Then we entered a wide, curving alley, bordered on each side by high latticework which cast shadows riddled with little flecks of light upon the sand. Clara looked eagerly between the lattice and the foliage. And despite myself, despite my sincere determination to henceforth close my eyes to the damnable spectacle, drawn by the strange magnet of horror, overwhelmed by the invincible vertigo of abominable sights, I too looked between the lattice and the foliage. And this is what we saw:

On the plateau of a broad, low hillock, on which the alley ended in a continuous and scarcely perceptible rise, there was a round space, artistically laid out like an arboretum, by skilful gardeners. Enormous, squat, of a dull bronze lugubriously streaked with red, the bell in the center of this space was hung by block and tackle to the top beam of a sort of black wood guillotine whose pillars were ornamented with gilded inscriptions and terrifying masks. Four men, stripped to the waist, their muscles taut and their skin so distended that they were no more than a mass of shapeless lumps, pulled on the rope of the tackle, and their combined and rhythmic efforts could scarcely lift or budge the heavy mass of metal, which at each pull gave off an almost inaudible sound, that sweet, pure, plaintive sound we had just heard, and whose vibrations were lost and died away among the flowers. The clapper, a heavy iron pestle, was then gently oscillating, but no longer touched the sonorous walls of the bell, tired of having sounded a poor devil's death-knell for so long a time. Under the cupola of the bell, two other men, their torsos rippling with sweat, their loins bare, and girdled with brown wool loin-cloths, were bending over something that could not be seen. Their chests with their protruding ribs and their lean flanks heaved like those of foundered horses.

All this could be vaguely seen, a little confused, a little jumbled, broken suddenly by the intervention of a thousand things, and then recomposed in the gaps of the foliage and the interstices in the lattice.

"We must hurry... we must hurry!" exclaimed Clara who, in order to walk faster, had closed her parasol and lifted her dress at the hips, with a bold gesture. 'The alley still curved, now flooded with sunlight, now shady, and it changed in appearance every moment, mingling with each floral beauty a more inexorable horror.

"Look carefully, my darling," said Clara. "Look all around. Here we are in the most beautiful and interesting section of the garden. Look! those flowers! oh, those flowers!" She indicated the bizarre plants which grew in a plot of earth where water could be seen gushing from all sides. I approached. On high stalks, flecked with black and scaly like snake-skins, there were enormous spathes, sort of bell-shaped trumpets the deep violet of putrefaction on the inside, and the greenish yellow of decomposition on the outer, which were like the split thoraxes of dead beasts. From the bottom of these trumpets there issued long sanguinolent spadices, assuming the form of monstrous phalluses. Attracted by the cadaverous odor these horrible plants gave off, flies hovered about in compact swarms and were swallowed by the spathes, which were lined from top to bottom with contractile, silky threads that enlaced them and held them prisoner more surely than a spider's web. And along the stalks, finger-like leaves contracted and twisted like the hands of tortured men.

"You see, my darling," instructed Clara, "these flowers are not the creation of any sickly soul, nor of a raving genius... they are natural. Didn't I tell you nature loved death!"

"Nature also creates monsters!"

"Monsters, monsters! But there are no monsters! What you call 'monsters' are superior forms, or forms simply beyond your understanding. Aren't the gods monsters? Isn't a man of genius a monster, like a tiger or a spider, like all individuals who live beyond social lies, in the dazzling and divine immorality of things? Why,

I too then—am a monster!"

We were then walking, between bamboo palisades, along which there ran hon-eysuckle, odorous jasmine, trumpet-flowers, arborescent mallow, and climbing hibiscus not yet in bloom. Moonseed embraced a stone column with its innumer-able lianas. On the top of the column grimaced the face of a hideous divinity whose ears spread like the wings of a bat, and whose hair ended in flaming horns, incarvillea, hemerocallis, morrea, and larkspur with leafless stems concealed its base with their little pink bells, their scarlet thyrses, their golden calyxes and pur-ple stars. Covered with ulcers and eaten by lice, a mendicant bonze who seemed to be the guardian of this structure, and who was training Touranian mongooses to make perilous leaps, insulted us as soon as we appeared.

"Dogs! dogs! dogs!"

We had to throw a few pieces of change to this fanatic, whose invective sur-passed all the outrageous obscenities which the indignation of the filthiest mind could conceive.

"I know him!" said Clara. "He's like all priests of all religions; he wants to frighten us into giving him a little money, but he's not a bad devil!"

From place to place in the recesses of the palisade which concealed verdant halls and beds of flowers, there were wooden benches equipped with chains and bronze collars, iron tables in the shapes of crosses,. blocks, gridirons, gibbets, automatic quartering machines, beds studded with cutting blades and bristling with iron spikes, stationary pillories, wooden horses, wheels, kettles and tanks suspended over extinguished fires—all the apparatus of sacrifice and torture, covered with blood, here dried and blackish, there sticky and red. Puddles of blood filled the hollow parts; long gobs of coagulated blood hung from disjointed machinery. Around these apparatus, the soil actually was wet with blood. Blood still starred the whiteness of the jasmine, marbled the pink coral of the honeysuckle and the mauve passion-flowers, and, bits of human flesh which had flown under the whips and leather thongs, were stuck here and there to the edges of the petals and leaves. Since I grew faint and grumbled at the sight of these puddles, which expanded and reached the middle of the path, Clara encouraged me in a gentle voice:

"This is nothing, yet, my darling... come along!" But it was difficult to proceed. Plants and trees, atmosphere and, earth were alive with flies, intoxicated insects, fierce and quarrelsome beetles, gorged mosquitoes. Around us all the fauna of the cadaver was hatching in myriads in the sun. Filthy maggots swarmed in the red pools, and dropped from the branches in soft clusters. The sand seemed to breathe and walk, lifted by the movement and pullulation of vermicular life. Deafened and blinded, we were halted at every step by these buzzing, multiplying swarms, and I was afraid for Clara—afraid of their deadly stings. And at times we had the hor-rible impression that our feet were sinking into the soaking earth, as though it had rained blood!

"This is nothing yet," repeated Clara, "come along with me!"

And here, to complete the drama, human faces appeared: squads of workmen who, with a nonchalant step, were coming to clean and repair the instruments of torture, for the hour of execution in the garden was over. They looked at us, doubtless astonished to encounter two people still standing at that time and in that place, two beings still alive, who still had their heads, their legs and arms. Further on, crouching on the earth in the posture of a grotesque china figure, we saw a big-bellied and good-natured potter who was varnishing freshly-baked flowerpots; near him, a weaver with indolent and exacting fingers was plaiting ingenious plant-shelters of supple reeds and rice-straws. A gardener was sharpening his grafting-tool on a grindstone, humming popular airs while an aged woman, chewing a betel-leaf and swaying her head in time, was placidly scouring a sort of iron maw whose sharp teeth still retained on their points some filthy human scraps. We also saw some children killing rats with sticks, and filling baskets with them. And along the palisades, hungry and fierce and dragging the imperial splendor of their tails in the bloody mud, peacocks—troupes of peacocks, pecked at the blood which had spurted into the hearts of the flowers, and clucking fiercely, snapped up the scraps of flesh stuck to the foliage. The oppressive odor of the slaughterhouse which persisted above all the other odors and dominated them, turned our stomachs and made us violently nauseous. Clara herself, fairy of the charnelhouse, angel of decomposition and rot, not so well sustained by her nerves, perhaps, had grown slightly pale. Sweat beaded her temples. I saw her eyes roll back and her legs grow weak.

"I'm cold!" she said. She gave me a glance of actual distress. Her nostrils, always distended like sails before the winds of death, had closed. I thought she was going to faint.

"Clara!" I begged. "You see very well it's impossible. You see there's a degree of horror which even you yourself cannot exceed." I stretched out my arms to her, but she refused them, and stiffening herself against sickness with all the indomitable energy of her frail organs:

"Are you crazy?" she said. "Come, my darling... faster... let's walk faster." However, she took out her flask, and smelled its salts.

"It's you who are all pale, and you walk like a drunken man. I'm not ill... I feel fine... and I'd like to sing." She began to sing:

Her clothes are summer gardens.

And temples...

But she had overestimated her strength, and her voice dried up in her throat. I thought this a good occasion to lead her back, persuade her, terrify her, perhaps. Vigorously, I attempted to draw her to me. "Clara! my little Clara! You must not defy your strength; you must not defy your heart. Let's go home, I beg you!" But she protested:

"No... no... leave me alone... say nothing... it's nothing. I'm happy!" And quickly, she slipped out of my embrace.

"You see! There isn't even any blood on my shoes." Then, annoyed:

"God, these flies are overwhelming! Why are there so many flies here? And these horrid peacocks—why don't they make them shut up?"

I tried to chase them away; some persisted in their bloody gleaning; others flew heavily off and, uttering more strident cries, perched not far from us on the top of the palisade and in the trees, from which their trains hung down like floods of material embroidered with dazzling jewels.

"Filthy beasts!" said Clara.

Thanks to the salts whose cordial odors she had breathed deeply, thanks especially to her implacable will not to faint, her face had already recovered its rosy tint, and her limbs their supple and vigorous movement. Then, in a firmer voice, she sang:

Her clothes are summer gardens.
And temples on festival-days.
Her firm and swelling breasts,
Gleam like a pair of golden vases,
Filled with intoxicating liquors and perfumes.
I have three mistresses...

After a moment of silence, she started to sing in a stronger voice, which drowned out the buzzing of the insects:

The hair of the third is plaited,
And rolled about her head.
And never has known the sweetness of perfumed oils.
That face which mirrors passion is deformed,
And her body is like a pig's...
And she always scolds and complains.
Her breasts and belly exhale a fishy odor
And her bed is more repugnant than a lapwing's nest.
And she is the one I love.

And I love her because there is something more mysteriously attractive than beauty: divine corruption.

Corruption in which the eternal heat of life resides.

Corruption in which the eternal renewal of metamorphoses unfolds. I have three mistresses.

While she was singing, while her voice was floating among the horrors of the garden, a cloud arose, very high, very far away. In the immensity of the sky, it was like a little pink bark, a tiny little bark with silken sails which grew as it progressed in its gentle glide. And when she had finished singing:

"Oh, the little cloud!" exclaimed Clara, suddenly joyful again. "Look how pretty it is, all pink against the azure! Don't you know it? Have you never seen it? Why,. it's a very mysterious little cloud... and perhaps even because it's not a little cloud at all. It appears every day at the same time, from God knows where.

And it's always alone, and always pink. It glides and glides and glides. Then it gets thinner, unravels, scatters, dissipates and melts into the firmament. And it's gone! And no one knows where it goes, any more than where it comes from! There are some very learned astronomers here who believe it's a genie. But I believe it's a wandering soul... a poor little bewildered soul, like mine. And speaking to herself, she added:"

"What if it's poor Annie's soul?"

For several minutes she contemplated the unknown cloud which was already growing pale, and little by little, fading away.

"There! there it's melting... melting. It's all over. No more little cloud! It's gone." She remained silent and fascinated, her eyes lost in the sky.

A light breeze had arisen, making a gentle shiver run through the trees, and the sun was less fierce and less overwhelming, its light growing magnificently copper towards the west and bathing the east in pearl-grey tones of infinite gradation. And the shadows of the kiosks and the great trees and the stone Buddhas lay slenderer, less defined, and altogether blue upon the lawns.

PART 8

We were near the bell. Very tall plum trees with twin blossoms, crowded together, intercepted our view of it. We discerned it from little shadows between the leaves and flowers, little decorative flowers, round and white like daisies.

The peacocks had followed us for some distance, brazen and wary at the same time, stretching their necks and trailing the splendid trains of their oscillated tails across the red sand. There were also some all white, their breasts speckled with bloody spots, and their cruel heads crowned with a broad fan-shaped crest, each feather of which, slender and stiff, bore at its tip what looked like a trembling droplet of pink crystal.

Iron tables, racks already set up, and sinister gear grew more numerous. In the shadow of a great tamarisk, we perceived a sort of rococo armchair. Its arms were made alternately of a saw and a steel blade, and its back and seat of iron spikes. A scrap of flesh hung from one of these spikes. Lightly, adroitly, Clara lifted it with the tip of her parasol and tossed it to the hungry peacocks who hurled themselves upon it, striking out fiercely with their beaks. For several moments there was a dazzling scramble, a clash of gems whose marvelous spectacle I loitered to admire despite my disgust. Perched in the neighboring trees, some lophophores, sacred pheasants, and great fighting cocks from the Malay Peninsula with damascene breasts, watched the conflict of the peacocks and cunningly awaited feeding-time.

Suddenly a wide gap opened in the wall of plum trees, a sort of light and flowery arch, and the bell was there before us—enormous and terrible before us. Its heavy beams, varnished black and decorated with gold inscriptions and red masks, seemed like the profile of a temple, and gleamed strangely in the sunlight. All around, the earth was covered with a layer of sand which muffled sound, and was surrounded by a wall of flowering plum trees blossoming with those heavy flowers which cover the entire length of their trunks with white bouquets. In the middle of this red and white circle, the bell was sinister to behold. It was somewhat like an abyss in the air, a hanging void which seemed to rise from earth to sky, and whose bottom, filled with silent shadows, could not be seen.

At that moment we understood what the two men were bending over—those men whose emaciated torsos and loins girdled with brown wool had appeared to us under the dome of the bell the moment we entered that part of the garden. They were bending over a corpse and unwrapping the ropes and leather thongs with which it had been firmly trussed. The corpse, the color of ochre clay, was entirely naked, and lay with its face to the ground. It was frightfully convulsed, the muscles bulging, its entire flesh violently disfigured, sunken here and bloated there, as by a tumor. You could see that the tortured man had struggled for a long time, vainly attempting to break his bonds, and that with the desperate and continuous effort both ropes and leather thongs had little by little sunk into his flesh, where they now made swellings of brown blood, coagulated pus, and greenish tissue. With one foot on the corpse, their backs arched, their arms taut as cables, the men were hauling on the bonds which they could not pull away without tearing out strips of flesh. And a rhythmic grunt issued from their throats, which ended shortly in a raucous whistle.

We approached.

The peacocks had halted. Augmented by new flocks, they now filled the circular alley and the flowered opening, which they dared not cross. Behind us, we heard their murmuring and subdued shuffling. In fact, it was like a crowd which had come running to the threshold of a temple, a dense, eager, impatient, smothering, and respectful crowd, their necks stretched, their eyes round; haggard and loquacious, watching the performance of a mystery they could not understand. We came still nearer.

"You see, my dear," said Clara, "how curious and unique it all is... and what magnificence! In what other country could you find a like spectacle? A torture-chamber decked out as for a ball; and this dazzling crowd of peacocks, acting as audience, atmosphere, rabble, and setting for the festival! Wouldn't you think we were transported beyond life, amid the imagery and poetry of the very old legends? Aren't you really astounded? It seems to me I'm always living in a dream here!"

Pheasants with radiant plumage and long jeweled necks soared and crossed above us. From place to place, several dared to perch on the tips of flowering stalks. Clara, who was following all the chance forms and colors of these fantastic flights, continued after a few minutes of charmed silence:

"Isn't it wonderful, my love, how the Chinese, so scorned by those who do not know them, are actually astounding people. No other race knows how to tame and domesticate nature with such painstaking skill. What unique artists! and what poets! See how that cadaver on the red sand takes on the tints of the old idols. Look at it carefully, for it's extraordinary, You'd think the vibrations of the bell, ringing wildly, had penetrated that body like some hard, compressing substance... that they'd forced the muscles out, made the veins burst, and twisted and ground the bones. A simple sound, so sweet to the ear, so deliciously musical, so touching to the mind, becoming something a thousand times more terrible and painful than all the old roly-poly's complicated instruments! Don't you think it's maddening? No, but conceive of this prodigious fact—that the very thing that can make amorous virgins walking in the country in the evening cry with ecstasy and divine melancholy, can also make men roar with pain, and kill a miserable human carcass under the most ineffable agony. I say it's genius! Ah, what a wonderful torture!... and so discreet, for it takes place in the shadows, and its horror, when you come to think of it, could not be equaled by any other. Besides, like the torture of the caress, it's very rare today, and you're lucky to have seen it on your first visit to the garden. They tell me the Chinese brought it from Korea, where it's very old, and where, it seems, it's still frequently employed. We'll go to Korea, if you like. The Koreans are inimitably fierce tortures—and they manufacture the most beautiful vases in the world, thick white vases, quite unique, which seem to have been dipped... ah, if you knew!... in baths of seminal fluid!"

Then, returning to the corpse:

"I'd like to know who this man was! For here they never prescribe the torture of the bell, except for high-class criminals: conspiring princes and high officials who no longer please the Emperor. It's an aristocratic and almost glorious torture." She shook my arm:

"You don't seem to be carried away by what I'm telling you. And you're not even listening to me! Just think—this bell, ringing and ringing. It's so sweet! When you bear it from a distance, it suggests some mystic sacrament, some joyous mass... baptisms... marriages. And it's the most terrifying of all deaths! I think it's wonderful. And you?" And as I did not answer:

"Yes... yes," she insisted. "Say it's wonderful! I want you to, I want you to! Be nice." Faced with my persistent silence, she made a little angry movement.

"How disagreeable you are!" she said. "You'll never be nice to me! What in the world can cheer you up? Ah, I don't want to love you any more. I have no more desire for you. Tonight you'll sleep alone, in the kiosk. I'll go and find my little Peach Blossom, who's so much nicer than you, and knows more about love than men."

I tried to stammer out something.

"No... no... never mind! It's over! I don't want to talk to you any more. And I'm sorry I didn't bring Peach Blossom. You're unbearable... and you make me sad. You make me stupid. It's odious! Here's a whole day wasted, which I'd planned to spend so thrillingly with you."

Her chatter and her voice irritated me. For some minutes I no longer noticed her beauty. Her eyes, her lips, her neck, her heavy golden hair, and the very ardor of her desire, and the very lustfulness of her sin, everything about her then seemed hideous to me. And from her gaping corsage, from the rosy nudity of her breast, where so often I had breathed, drunk, and feasted on the intoxication of such heady perfume, there arose an exhalation of putrefied flesh, that little mass of putrefied flesh which was her soul. Several times I had been tempted to interrupt her with a violent outburst... shut her mouth with my fists... wring her neck. I felt so savage a hatred rising in me against this woman, that seizing her arm roughly, I cried out in an unrestrained voice:

"Shut up! Oh, shut up! Don't ever talk to me again—never! For I'd like to kill you, you devil! I ought to kill you, and then throw you to the dogs, you beast!" In spite of my excitement, I was afraid of my own words. But to make them irrevocable after all, I repeated them, bruising her arm with my frantic hands: "Beast! beast! beast!"

Clara made not the slightest movement to draw back, not even a flutter of the lids. She thrust out her throat and offered her breast. Her face lit up with an unknown and resplendent joy. Simply, slowly, with infinite sweetness, she said:

"Well, kill me darling! I'd love to be killed by you, dear little darling!"

That was the only flash of rebellion in the long and painful passivity of my submission. It died out as swiftly as it had flared up. Ashamed of the insultingly vile epithet I had just uttered, I released Clara's arm, and all the anger due to my nervous excitation suddenly melted in a great dejection.

"Ah, you see," said Clara, who did not care to take further advantage of my pitiful defeat and her too easy triumph, "you haven't even the courage for that, and it would be beautiful. Poor baby!" And as though nothing had happened between us, she began to follow the frightful drama of the bell again, with passionate interest.

During this short scene the two men had been resting. They seemed exhausted. Emaciated, panting, their ribs bulging beneath their skin; their thighs fleshless, they no longer seemed human. The sweat flowed, as from a spout, from the points of their mustaches, and their sides heaved like those of beasts hard pressed by dogs. But a guard suddenly appeared, whip in hand. He yelled, and with blow after blow, lashed the bony loins of the two wretches, who set to work again, howling.

Frightened by the cracking of the whip, the peacocks screamed and flapped their wings. They fled in tumult, a whirling mass in panic-stricken disorder. Then, reassured little by little, they came back one by one, couple by couple, group by group, to take their places under the floral arch, swelling the splendor of their throats still more, and darting even fiercer glances upon the scene of death. The pheasants, red, yellow, blue and green, still wheeling over the white circle, embroidered the luminous ceiling of the sky with dazzling silks and soft changing patterns.

Clara called the guard, and engaged him in a brief conversation in Chinese which she related to me as fast as he replied.

"These are the poor devils who rang the bell. Forty-two hours without a drink, without a single rest! Can you imagine it! And how is it they aren't dead too? I know very well the Chinese aren't made like us, and that in fatigue and physical pain they have extraordinary endurance. I too wanted to know how long a Chinese could work without taking nourishment. Twelve days, darling... they only drop at the end of the twelfth day! It's unbelievable! It's true that the work I imposed on him was nothing like this. I had him plow the earth, in the sun." She'd forgotten my insults and her voice was amorous and caressing again, like when she told me love-stories. She continued:

"For you don't question, darling, the violent, continuous, and superhuman effort it takes to set in action and work the clapper of the bell, do you? Even many of the strongest succumb at it. A ruptured artery... a lesion of the loins... and it's all over! They fall dead suddenly, on the bell! And those who don't die of it in their tracks get diseases from which they never recover. Look how swollen and bloody their hands are from the friction of the rope! Besides, it seems that these are convicts, too. They die in killing, and the two tortures balance each other, see! All the same, you must be kind to these wretches... when the guard goes away, won't you give them a few taels?" And returning to the corpse:

"Ah, you know... I know him now. He was a big city banker... was very rich and stole from everyone. But he wasn't sentenced to the torture of the bell for that. The guard doesn't know exactly why. They say he negotiated treacherously with the Japanese. They have to give some reason."

Scarcely had she uttered these words, than we heard some hollow moans, like stifled sobbing. They came from directly in front of us, from behind the white wall along which petals were falling off and slowly dropping onto the red sands. Tears and flowers falling!

"It's his family," Clara explained. "It's there according to the custom, waiting for them to deliver the body of the tortured man." At that moment the two exhausted men who, by a miracle of will, were still standing up, were turning the body over. Simultaneously, Clara and I uttered a single cry. And clasped to me, tearing my shoulder with her nails:

"Oh, darling! darling! darling!" she cried; an exclamation by which she always expressed the intensity of her emotion at the approach of horror, as well as love. And we looked at the cadaver, and with the same horrified motion stretched our necks toward the cadaver, and we could not tear our eyes away from the cadaver.

On its convulsed face, on which all the contracted muscles were outlined, frightful grimaces and hideous angles stood out, the twisted mouth revealing the teeth and gums, mimicked the frightful laugh of a madman, a laugh which death had stiffened, fixed and, so to say, modeled into all the folds of the skin. The two staring eyes darted a sightless glance at us, but their expression of the most terrifying insanity remained, and so prodigiously sneering and so fitfully mad was this stare, that never in the cells of an asylum had I been destined to see its like in the eyes of a living man.

Observing all these muscular displacements in the corpse, all these deviations of the tendons, all these projections of the bones, and on the face, this grin and this dementia of the eyes surviving death, I understood how much more horrible than any other torture must be the agony of a man lying forty-two hours in his bonds under the bell. Neither the dismembering knife, nor the red, burning iron, nor the ripping pincers, nor the wedges which spread the joints, crack the articulations, or split the bones like pieces of wood, can work greater ravages on organs of living flesh and fill the brain with more horror than this sound of an invisible and immaterial bell, combining in itself all the known instruments of torture, infuriating all the sensitive and thinking parts of an individual at the same time, and fulfilling the office of more than a hundred executioners.

The two men had started to pull on the ropes again, their throats wheezing and their sides heaving more rapidly. But their strength was gone, and flowed from their limbs in rivulets of sweat. They could scarcely stand erect now, and with their stiff and ankylosed fingers, pull on the leather thongs.

"Dogs!" howled the guard.

A blow of the whip wrapped their loins and did not even make them tense themselves against the pain. It seemed that, with their nerves unstrung, all feeling had disappeared. Their knees, giving and trembling more and more, now knocked against each other. What muscles remained under the flayed skin contracted in tetanic movements. Suddenly one of them, at the peak of exhaustion, gave a little raucous moan and throwing his arms forward, fell beside the corpse, his face against the earth, spewing a flood of black blood.

"Up! coward! Up! dog!" the guard shouted again. Four times the lash hissed and snapped on the man's back. The pheasants perched on the flowering stalks flew off with a great whirring of wings. Behind us, I heard the startled chatter of the peacocks. But the man did not get up. He did not stir again, and the pool of blood grew wider on the sand. The man was dead!

Then I dragged Clara away. Her little fingers dug into my skin. I felt very pale, and walked and stumbled like a drunkard. "It's too much... too much!" I constantly repeated. And, Clara, who followed docilely, also repeated:

"Ah, you see, my darling! I knew. Did I lie to you?"

We reached an alley which led to the central pond, and the peacocks which had followed us that far left suddenly and scattered with a great noise across the bushes and lawns of the gardens.

This very broad alley was bordered on either side by dead trees, immense tamarinds whose great bare branches crisscrossed in stern arabesques against the sky. A niche had been dug in every trunk. The majority were empty, while some enclosed the bodies of men and women, violently distorted and subjected to hideous and shameful tortures. Before the occupied niches, a sort of clerk in a black gown stood gravely, a writing desk swung in front of him, and a register in his hands.

"This is the alley of the accused," Clara told me. "And these people you see standing here are only present to take down the confessions which prolonged suffering might drag from these wretches. They rarely confess, preferring to die like this rather than prolong their agony in the cages of the bagnio and finally perish under other tortures. Generally the tribunals do not make much use of accusations, except in political crimes. They judge in groups, in batches, willy-nilly. Besides, you see there are not many accused, and the majority of the niches are empty. It's none the less true that the idea is ingenious. I really believe they got it from Greek mythology. It's a horrible adaptation of that charming fable of the hamadryads, imprisoned in their trees.

Clara approached a tree where a young woman was breathing her last. She was suspended by her wrists from an iron hook, and the wrists were clasped between two blocks of wood pressed together with great force. A knotted rope of coconut fiber covered with pulverized pimento and mustard and soaked in a salt solution, was wound about her arms.

"They keep that rope ort,"' my friend condescended to remark, "until the arms are swollen to four times their natural size. Then they take it off, and the sores it produces often burst, making hideous wounds. They frequently die of it, but never recover."

"But if the accused is found innocent?" I asked. "Oh well... " said Clara.

Another woman in another niche had her limbs spread, or rather, torn apart; her neck and arms were clamped in iron collars. Her eyelids, nostrils, lips and other parts were rubbed with red pepper, and two thumbscrews crushed her nipples. Farther on a young man was suspended by means of a rope passed under his armpits; a great block of stone hung from his shoulders, and you could hear the cracking of his joints. Still another, his back arched, balanced by an iron wire which bound his neck to his two big toes, was crouching with sharp-pointed stones in the bend of his knees. The niches in the trunks were becoming empty. Only from place to place there was a man bound, crucified, or hanging, whose eyes were closed and seemed to be asleep—and perhaps was dead. Clara spoke no more, and no longer explained anything. She listened to the heavy flight of the vultures circling above the interlacing branches, and the cawing of crows sailing through the sky in countless flocks. The lugubrious alley of tamarinds ended on a broad terrace flowering with peonies, from which we descended to the pond.

The irises lifted their strangely flowered stalks above the water, their petals the color of old sandstone vases, precious, blood-purple enamels, sinister purples, blue flamed with orange ochre, velvet blacks, and their calilyxes sulphur-colored. Some, immense and twisted, looked like cabalistic characters. The water-lilies and nelumbos spread their great swooning blossoms on the golden water, and looked to me like severed, floating heads. We remained some minutes leaning on the balustrade of the bridge, looking silently at the water. All enormous carp whose golden snout alone could be seen, slept under a leaf, and between the Indian grass and the reeds smaller carp swam back and forth, like evil thoughts in a woman's brain.

PART 9

And so the day is ending. The sky becomes red, striped by broad, surprisingly translucent emerald bands. It is the hour when the flowers take on a mysterious brilliance, a glitter both hard and restrained. They flame everywhere, as though they gave the evening atmosphere its light—all the sunlight with which their pulp has been saturated during the day. Between the heightened green of the lawns and these flaming bands, the paths of pulverized brick seem like streams of incandescent lava. The birds are silent in the branches; the insects have hushed their humming and are dying or asleep. The nocturnal butterflies and bats alone begin to wander in the air. Everywhere, from the sky to the trees, and from the trees to the earth, there is silence. And I also feel it penetrate me, chilling me like death. A flock of cranes descends the slope of the lawn and forms a ring around the pool, not far from us. I can hear the patter of their feet in the tall grass, and the dry clicking of their bills. Then, standing on one leg, motionless, their heads beneath their wings, they seem like bronze decorations. And the golden-snouted carp which was sleeping under a nelumbo leaf, tacks about in the water, then plunges and disappears, leaving broad circles on the surface which gently sway the closed calyxes of the water-lilies, then broaden and are lost among the tufts of iris whose diabolic flowers, strangely defined, inscribe, under the evening magic, symbolic signs out of the Book of Fate. Above the water an enormous arum-lily spreads the trumpet of its greenish flower mottled with brown spots, and wafts to us the strong odor of a corpse. For a long time the flies swarm persistently and intently about its carrion calyx.

Leaning on the railing of the bridge, her forehead barred with shadow, her eyes intent, Clara looks at the water. The reflection of the setting sun glows on the back of her neck. Her flesh is slack and her lips compressed. She is grave and very sad. She looks at the water, but her glance goes further and deeper than the water; it sinks perhaps, towards something more impenetrable and blacker than the bottom of this pond; perhaps it plumbs her soul, the gulf of her soul which, in eddies of flame and blood, unfolds the monstrous blossoms of its desire. What is she really looking at? What is she thinking of? I do no know. Perhaps thinking of nothing. Somewhat weary, her nerves bruised and torn under the lash of too many sins, she is silent, that is all. Unless by a last effort of cerebration, she is gathering all the memories and images of this horrible day, to offer them as a bouquet of red flowers to her sex. I don't know.

I dare not speak to her. She frightens me, and she also troubles me to the very

depths of my being, by her immobility and silence. Does she really exist? I wonder, somewhat fearfully. Was she not born of my debauchery and fever? Is she not
one of those impossible visions to which nightmares give birth? One of those
criminal temptations such as lust stirs in the imagination of those invalids called
assassins and murderers? Might she not be nothing more than my soul, escaped
from me despite myself and materialized in the form of sin? No... for I can touch
her. My hand recognized the admirable, living realities of her body. Through the
scant silky material which covers it, her skin burned my fingers. And Clara did
not tremble at their contact; she did not swoon, as she often has, at their caress. I
desire her and I hate her. I would like to take her in my arms and embrace her till
she smothered, till she was crushed and I could drink her death from her gushing
veins. In a voice first threatening and then submissive, I exclaim:

"Clara! Clara! Clara!"

Clara does not reply, she does not budge. She still looks at the water which is
growing darker and darker; but I really do not believe she is looking at the water,
nor the red reflection of the sky in the water, nor the flower, nor herself. Then I
draw away a little, in order not to see her any longer, or touch her, and I turn
towards the disappearing light, towards the light which only remains in the sky as
a great ephemeral glow, soon little by little to melt away and go out in the night.

Shadow descends on the garden, trailing its blue veils, lightly over the bare
lawns, heavily on the sharply outlined bushes. The white flowers on the cherry
trees and peach trees, now a lunar white, seem to glide and wander and assume
the weird aspects of phantoms. And the gallows and stakes lift their sinister
columns and black framework in the oriental sky, blue as steel. Horror! Above a
bush, against the dying purple of the evening, turning and turning on the stakes,
slowly turning in the void and swaying like flowers whose stalks would be visible at night, I can see the black silhouettes of five tortured men.

"Clara! Clara! Clara!"

My voice does not reach her. Clara does not reply, does not budge, does not turn.
She remains bending over the water, over the gulf of water. And just as she does
not hear me, no more does she hear the moans, cries, and death-rattles of all those
dying in the garden.

I feel something like a powerful oppression, like an immense fatigue after
marching and marching across fever-laden jungles, or by the shores of deadly
lakes—and I am flooded by discouragement, so that it seems I shall never be able
to escape from myself again. At the same time, my brain is heavy and troubles me.
It feels as though an iron band were clasping my temples, tight enough to burst
my skull.

Then, little by little, my thoughts abandon the garden, the torture-arenas, the
agony beneath the bell, the trees haunted by pain, the bloody and devouring flowers. They are trying to burst through the setting of this charnel-house, penetrate to
pure light, knock once more upon the gates of life. Alas, the gates of life never

swing open except upon death, never open except upon the palaces and gardens of death. And the universe appears to me like an immense, inexorable torture-garden. Blood everywhere and, where there is most life, horrible tormentors who dig your flesh, saw your bones, and retract your skin with sinister, joyful faces.

Ah, yes! the Torture Garden! Passions, appetites, greed, hatred, and lies; law, social institutions, justice, love, glory, heroism, and religion: these are its monstrous flowers and its hideous instruments of eternal human suffering. What I saw today, and what I heard, exists and cries and howls beyond this garden, which is no more than a symbol to me of the entire earth. I have vainly sought a respite in quietude and repose in death, and I can find them nowhere.

I should like, yes, I should like to be reassured, cleanse my soul and brain with old memories, with the memory of friendly, familiar faces. I call Europe and its hypocritical civilization to my aid, and Paris—my joyful, laughing Paris. But it is the face of Eugene Mortain I see grimacing on the shoulders of the fat loquacious executioner who, at the foot of the gallows, in the flowers, was cleaning his saws and scalpels. These are the eyes, the mouth, the limp and pendant cheeks of Mme. G— I see bending over the wooden horses, and her rapacious hands I see touching and caressing the iron jaws, gorged with human flesh. On all those men and women I loved or thought I loved, little indifferent, frivolous souls, the indelible red stain now lies. And these are the judges, soldiers, and priests who everywhere, in the churches, barracks and temples of justice persist in the work of death. And it is in the individual man, and the man-crowd, and it is in the beast, the plant, the element; it is in all nature in fact which, urged on by the cosmic forces of love, rushes to murder, hoping thus to find beyond life satiation for the furious desires of life which devour it and overflow it in jets of filthy scum! Just now I wondered who Clara was and whether she really existed. Does she exist! Why Clara! Clara *is* life, the actual presence of life and all of life!

"Clara! Clara! Clara!"

She does not reply, she does not budge, she does not turn around. A thicker blue and silver mist rises from the lawns and the pond and envelops the bushes, shrouding the gallows. And it seems to me that an odor of blood, an odor of the corpse rises with it—an incense that invisible censers, swung by invisible hands, offer to the deathless glory of death and to the everlasting glory of Clara!

On the other bank of the pool, behind me, the gecko begins to sound the hours. Another gecko answers... then another... then, another, at regular intervals. They are like bells calling and conversing as they sing, festal bells of an extraordinarily pure timbre, crystalline and sweetly sonorous, so sweet they suddenly dissipate the nightmare shapes which haunt the garden and: give security to the silence, and the charm of a white dream to the night. These notes, so clear, so inexpressibly clear, now evoke in me thousands and thousands of nocturnal landscapes, in which my lungs can breathe, and in which my thought quickens. In a few moments I have forgotten that I am beside Clara, that about me the soil and flowers actually are wet with blood, and I see myself wandering across the silvery night in the midst of the fantastic rice-fields of Annam.

"Let's go home!" says Clara.

This abrupt, aggressive, and weary voice recalls me to reality. Clara is before me. Her crossed legs are outlined beneath the clinging folds of her dress, and she leans on the handle of her parasol. In the twilight, her lips shine like a little light shielded by a pink shade, in a great closed room. As I do not stir, she speaks again:

"Well, I'm waiting!"

I try to take her arm but She refuses.

"No... no. Let's walk side by side."

"The road is long from here to the river. Take my arm, I beg you."

"No... thank you. Be quiet; oh, be quiet!"

"Clara! You are not the same."

"If you want to please me, be quiet. I don't like to be spoken to at this time."

Her voice is dry, cutting and imperious. Now we are leaving. We cross the bridge, she first and I behind her, and we enter little alleys which meander across the lawns. Clara walks with abrupt steps, jerkily, and with difficulty. And such is the invulnerable beauty of her body that these efforts do not break its full, harmonious, and supple lines. Her hips retain a divinely voluptuous swing. Even when her mind is far from love, when it stiffens, writhes and protests against love, it is still love—all the forms, intoxication, and ardors of love which animate it and, so to speak, mould this predestined body. There is not an attitude about her, not a gesture, not a quiver, not a swish of her dress or a wave of her hair, which does not cry love, which does not ooze love, which does not shower love about her upon every being and on everything. The sand of the alley cries out beneath her little feet, and I hear the noise of the sand, like a cry of desire, like a kiss, in which I distinguish, clear and rhythmical, the name which is everywhere—which was in the creaking of the stake and the death rattle of the dying men, and fills the twilight now with its exquisite, funereal murmur that fades and rises:

"Clara! Clara! Clara!"

The gecko is silent now, to hear that name more clearly. Everything is silent.

The twilight is enchanting, infinitely sweet, and with a caressing coolness which intoxicates. We walk amid perfumes. We brush by marvelous flowers, more marvelous for being scarcely visible, which bow before us and greet us on our way, like mysterious fairies. Nothing remains of the horror of the garden; only its beauty remains, trembles and heightens as the night falls more and more deliciously about us.

I feel recovered. It seems my fever is gone. My limbs become lighter, stronger, and more elastic. As I walk along, my fatigue vanishes, and I feel something like a violent need of love rising in me. I have caught up to Clara and I walk beside her... quite near her... excited by her. But Clara's face is no longer sinful, as when she was chewing the thalictrum blossom and passionately peppering her lips with its bitter pollen. The frozen expression of her face belies all the sensuous ardor of her body. At least, as far as I can see, it really seems that the lust which trembled with so strange a flame in: her eyes and swooned upon her mouth, has disappeared, completely disappeared from her mouth and eyes, together with the bloody images of torture in the garden. In a trembling voice, I ask her:

"You're angry at me, Clara? You detest me?"

She replies in an irritable voice:

"No! no! That's beside the point, my friend. I beg you, please be quiet. You don't know how much you fatigue me!"

I insist:

"Yes! yes! I can see you detest me... and it's frightful! I feel like weeping!"

"God, you annoy me! Be quiet... and weep if it will give you any pleasure. But be quiet!" And as we pass the place where we stopped to talk to the old executioner, hoping by my stupid persistence to bring back a smile to Clara's dead lips, I say:

"Do you remember the roly-poly, my love? How funny he was, with his gown covered with blood, and his instrument-case, and his red fingers, darling... and his theories about the sex of flowers? Do you remember? Sometimes twenty males are required for; the delight of a single female."

This time a shrug of her shoulders is her reply. She does not even deign to be irritated by my words. Then, urged by crude desire, I clumsily try to embrace Clara, and with brutal hands I grasp her breasts.

"I want you... here... you hear me?... in this garden... in this silence... at the foot of these gallows." My voice is panting and a vile slaver flows from my mouth, and together with that slaver, abominable words... the words she loves!

With a twist of the loins, Clara releases herself from my clumsy embrace, and in a voice, in which there is anger, irony and also lassitude and enervation:

"God! how frightfully boring you are, if you only knew... and ridiculous, my poor friend! What a common goat you are! Leave me alone. In a little while, if you insist, you can work out your dirty desires on the harlots. You're really too ridiculous!"

Ridiculous! Yes, I feel ridiculous... and I become resigned to be quiet. I would not care to tumble into her silence again, like a heavy stone falling in a lake where swans are sleeping under the moon!

PART 10

The sampan, all illuminated with red lanterns, was waiting for us at the wharf of the bagnio. A Chinese woman with a coarse face, dressed in blouse and trousers of black silk, her arms bare and loaded with heavy gold bracelets, her ears hung with big gold hoops, was holding the hawser. Clara jumped into the bark, and I followed her.

"Where do you want to go?" the Chinese woman asked in English. Clara answered in a jerky, trembling voice:

"Anywhere you wish... it doesn't matter where... on the river. You know very well." I noticed then that she was very pale. Her pinched nostrils, her drawn features, and her vague eyes expressed great suffering. The Chinese woman nodded her head vaguely at me.

"Yes... yes, I know," she said. Her thick lips were corroded by the betel-nut, and there was a bestial harshness in her glance. As she was still muttering words I did not understand:

"Come, Ki-Pai," commanded Clara in an abrupt tone, "shut up, and do as I tell you. Besides, the gates of the city are closed."

"The gates of the garden are open—"

"Do as I tell you."

Dropping the hawser, the Chinese woman grasped the sculling oar with a vigorous movement and handled it skillfully. We glided over the water.

The night was very balmy. We breathed a warm but infinitely fragrant air. The water sang about the prow of the sampan, and the view on the river was like a great festival.

On the opposite shore, and on our right and left, variegated lanterns lit up the masts, sails, and crowded decks of the boats. A strange murmur in the air—cries, chants, and music—came from them, as from a holiday crowd. The water was quite black, a dull, velvety black, with occasional dull, ripply gleams and no other bright lights than the shattered red and green reflections of the lanterns that illuminated the sampans with which the stream was literally jammed at this hour. Beyond a somber space in the dark sky, rising between the black masses of the trees, the city lay in the distance with *its* mounting terraces lit like an immense red brazier, like a fiery mountain.

As we went farther off we could make out, less distinctly, the high walls of the bagnio from which, at every round of the night watchmen, their swaying torches shot blinding triangles of light onto the stream and over the countryside.

Clara had disappeared under the canopy which transformed this bark into a sort of cozy boudoir, lined with silk and breathing of love. Violent perfumes burned in a very ancient wrought-iron vase—a naive, synthetic image of an elephant whose four massive, barbaric feet rested on delicate interlacing roses. There were voluptuous prints on the hangings—boldly lustful scenes, executed strangely, cleverly, and magnificently. The frieze of the canopy, a precious piece in colored wood, exactly reproduced a fragment of that mural in the subterranean temple of Elephanta, which the archeologists, in accordance with Brahman traditions, modestly call: The Union of the Rooks. A broad deep mattress of embroidered silk occupied the center of the bark, and from the ceiling there hung a lantern with phallic inserts, a lantern partly draped with orchids which shed the mysterious twilight of an alcove or a sanctuary over the interior of the sampan.

Clara threw herself on the cushions. She was extraordinarily pale, and her body trembled, shaken by nervous spasms. I tried to take her hands, and they were icy.

"Clara! Clara!" I implored, "what's the matter with you? What are you suffering from? Speak to me!" She replied in a raucous voice which issued painfully from her contracted throat:

"Leave me alone. Don't touch me... don't talk to me. I'm sick." Her pallor, her bloodless lips, and her rasping voice frightened me. I thought she was going to die. Terrified, I called the Chinese woman to my aid:

"Quick! quick! Clara's dying! Clara's dying! Come quick!"

But having parted the curtains and shown her chimera's face, Ki-Pai shrugged her shoulders and exclaimed brutally:

"That's nothing. She's always like that when she comes back from down there." And grumbling, she returned to her oar.

Under Ki-Pai's muscular exertions, the bark, lifted in the water, slid more rapidly over the stream. We crossed in front of sampans like our own, from whose canopies with their closed curtains there came songs, the sound of kisses, laughter, and the groans of love, which mingled with the lapping of the water and the distant, almost smothered reverberation of tom-toms and gongs. In a few minutes we had reached the other shore and for a long time glided by black, deserted hulks, and others lit and crowded; low dives, porter's teahouses, flower-boats for sailors and the riffraff of the port. Through portholes and lighted windows I caught fleeting scenes—strange painted faces, lewd dances, wild debauchery, faces of people under the influence of opium. Clara remained insensible to all that was taking place around her, both in the silken bark or on the stream. Her face was pressed into the pillow, and she chewed on it. I tried to make her breathe the smelling-salts. Three times she pushed the flask away with an exhausted, heavy gesture. Her throat bare, her breasts bursting the torn material of her corsage, her legs tense and vibrant as the strings of a viol, she was breathing with difficulty. I didn't know what to do; I didn't know what to say. And I bent over her, with her agonizing soul, full of its tragic incertitudes and countless troubles. To reassure myself that it was really a passing crisis, that nothing in her had broken the springs of life, I grasped her wrist. Under my hand her pulse beat rapidly, light, and regular as the heart of a little bird or a little child. From time to time a sigh escaped her lips, a long and painful sigh which lifted and swelled her rosy breast. Trembling, I murmured in a low and very gentle voice:

"Clara! Clara! Clara!"

She did not hear me, did not see me, and her face was hidden in the pillow. Her hat had slipped from her hair whose red-gold, under the glow of the lantern, took on the tones of old mahogany, and projecting from her dress, her feet, clad in yellow leather, still were spotted here and there with bloody mud.

"Clara! Clara! Clara!"

Nothing but the song of the water and the distant music and, between the curtains of the canopy, down there, the fiery mountain of the terrible city, and nearer, the red, green, alert, and sinuous reflections diving about in the black stream like slender, luminous eels.

There was a slight shock, the Chinese woman called, and we drew up beside a sort of long terrace, the illuminated terrace of a flower-boat clamorous with music and excitement. Ki-Pai moored the bark to some iron hooks in front of a ladder whose red rungs dipped into the water. Two enormous, round lanterns gleamed on top of poles decked with fluttering yellow pennants.

"Where are we?" I asked.

"We are where she ordered me to bring you," replied Ki-Pai in a surly tone of voice, "where she spends the night when she comes back from down there." I suggested:

"Wouldn't it be better to take her home, in her condition?"

Ki-Pai replied:

She's always like that after the bagnio. And then, the town is closed, and to get to the palace through the gardens is too far now, and too dangerous." And contemptuously, she added: "She's all right here. She's well known here."

I gave in.

"Then help me," I commanded, "and don't be rough with her."

Very gently, with infinite precaution, Ki-Pai and I took Clara in our arms, who offered no more resistance than a dead woman. Supporting her, or rather, carrying her, we got her out of the bark with difficulty, and helped her up the ladder. She was cold and heavy. Her head was thrown slightly back and her thick and sinuous hair, entirely undone, tumbled about her shoulders in fiery waves. Grasping Ki-Pai's coarse neck with a limp hand, and almost fainting, she uttered vague little moans and blurted out inarticulate little words, like a child. And panting slightly under my friend's weight, I groaned:

"If only she doesn't die, my God! If only she doesn't die!" Ki-Pai sneered with her fierce mouth:

"Die! She! There's no suffering in her body... only corruption!"

We were received at the top of the ladder by two women whose eyes were made up, and whose golden nakedness gleamed through the light, diaphanous veils which draped them. They had shameful jewels in their hair, jewels on their wrists and fingers, jewels on their ankles and bare feet, and their skin, rubbed with fine essences gave off scents of a garden. One of them clapped her hands joyfully:

"Why it's our little friend!" she cried. "I told you she'd come, the darling. She always does. Quick... quick... lay her on the bed, the darling."

She indicated a sort of mattress, or rather litter, stretched out against the wall, and we laid Clara on it. She no longer moved. Under her frightfully open lids, only the whites of her eyes showed. Then the Chinese woman with the painted eyes bent over Clara, and in a deliciously rhythmic voice, as though she were singing, said:

"Little, little friend of my breasts and my soul... how beautiful you are like that! You are as beautiful as a young girl dead. However, you are not dead. You are going to revive, little friend of my lips, revive under my caresses and the perfumes of my mouth."

She moistened Clara's forehead with a violent perfume, and made her inhale the salts:

"Yes, yes! dear little soul. You have fainted... and you cannot hear me! and you cannot feel my gentle fingers... but your heart beats, beats, beats. And love gallops in your veins like a young horse... love bounds in your veins like a young tiger."

She turned to me:

"You must not be sad, because she has always fainted when she comes here. In a few minutes we'll cry with delight over her happy burning flesh."

And I stood there, inert, silent, my limbs leaden, my chest oppressed as in a nightmare. I had no further sensation of reality. All I had seen—mutilated visions rising from the surrounding shadows and the depths of the stream, then diving in again to reappear soon in fantastic shapes—terrified me. The long terrace hanging in the night, with its red-lacquered balustrades and slender columns supporting the bold slant of its roof, its garlands of lanterns alternating with garlands of flowers, was filled with a chattering, stirring and extraordinarily colorful crowd. A hundred painted glances fastened upon us, a hundred painted-mouths whispered words I could not hear, but in which I seemed to hear Clara's name ceaselessly repeated perhaps only in my mind:

"Clara! Clara! Clara!"

And naked bodies, clasped bodies, tattooed arms loaded with gold bracelets, bellies and breasts, all twisted under their diaphanous, flying scarves. And in all this, around all this, above all this, there rose cries, laughter, songs, the notes of a flute, odors of tea and precious woods, the powerful aroma of opium, and breaths heavy with perfume. The intoxication of dream, debauch, torture and crime—all these hands, mouths, breasts, and all this living flesh came hurling upon Clara, to possess her dead flesh!

I could not make a move or utter a word. At my side a very young and pretty Chinese girl, almost a child, with eyes both candid and provocative, was hawking strangely indelicate objects in a basket—shameless ivories, rose-colored rubber verges and illustrated books in which the thousand complicated joys of love were painted.

"Love! love! who wants love? I have love for everyone!"

However I bent over Clara...

"You must bring her to my room," commanded the Chinese girl with painted eyes. Two powerful men lifted the litter, and mechanically, I followed them. Guided by the courtesan, they went through a wide corridor, sumptuous as a temple. On the right and left, doors opened upon great rooms spread with mats and lit by soft pink lights draped with muslin. Presiding over the thresholds, symbolic animals thrust out enormous and terrible organs, hermaphroditic divinities gave themselves to each other or straddled impassioned monsters. And perfumes burned in precious bronze vases. A silk portiere embroidered with peach blossoms parted and two women's heads were thrust through the opening. Watching us pass by, one of these women said: "Who's dead?" The other replied:

"No! No one's dead. Can't you see it's the woman from the Torture Garden." And Clara's name, whispered from mouth to mouth, from bed to bed, and room to room, soon filled the flower-boat like some monstrous jest. It even seemed to me that the metal monsters repeated it in their ecstasy, howling it in their delirium of bloody passion.

"Clara! Clara! Clara!"

Here, I caught a glimpse of a young man stretched out on a bed. A little opium-lamp was burning within reach of his hand. In his strangely dilated eyes there was something like an agonizing ecstasy. Before him, mouth to mouth, and body to body, naked women clasping each other danced sacred dances while musicians, crouched behind a screen, blew into short flutes. There, seated in a circle or lying on the floor-mat in dissolute poses, their debauched faces sadder than the faces of the tortured, other women were waiting. At each door we passed there was moaning—panting voices, gestures of the damned, crushed and twisted bodies—a grimacing anguish sometimes howling under the lash of fierce passions and barbaric abuse. Guarding the entrance to one door, I saw a bronze group the mere arabesque of whose lines made me shudder with horror. An octopus, embracing the body of a virgin with its tentacles, was amorously crushing her. And I felt I was in a place of torture, not a house of joy and love.

The jam in the corridor became so great that for several seconds we were obliged to halt in the threshold of a room—the largest of them all—which differed from the others by its decorations and its sinister red lighting. At first, I only saw the women—a tangle of furious flesh and living scarves—women abandoning themselves to frantic dances and demoniac possession, around a sort of idol whose massive bronze, of a very ancient patina, rose in the center of the room and towered to the ceiling. Then the idol itself became clear, and I recognized it as that terrible idol known as the Idol of the Seven Verges. Three heads armed with red horns, coiffed with hair in twisted flames, crowned a single body, or rather a single belly, based on an enormous, pagan and phallic-form pillar. All around this pillar, at the exact point the monstrous belly ended, seven bronze verges thrust forth, to which the dancing women offered flowers and furious caresses. And the red glow of the room gave diabolic life to the jade balls which served as the Idol's eyes. At the moment we started again I witnessed a frightful spectacle whose infernal, shuddering horror it is impossible for me to describe. Shouting and howling, seven women suddenly hurled themselves upon the seven bronzes. The Idol, embraced by all this raving flesh, vibrated under the multiple shocks of this possession and the kisses which rang out like the blows of a battering ram on the iron gates of a besieged city. Then there was a maddened clamor about the Idol, an insanity of savage abandon, a storm of bodies so frantically clasped and welded to each other that they assumed the fierce appearance of a massacre, resembling the carnage of those condemned men in their iron cages fighting over Clara's scrap of putrid meat! In that atrocious second I understood that desire can attain the darkest human terror and give an actual idea of hell and its horror.

And it seemed to me that all these shocks, all these panting voices, all these groans, all these bites and the Idol itself, had only one word—a single word—to express and belch their rage of insatiability and the torture of their impotence:

"Clara!"

When we had reached the room and deposited Clara, still unconscious, on a bed, I once more became aware of myself and where I was. These chants, debauches, sacrifices, devitalizing perfumes and impure contacts which further soiled the sleeping soul of my friend, flooded me with an overwhelming shame even more powerful than my horror. I had great difficulty in chasing away the curious and talkative women who had followed us, not only from the bed on which we had laid Clara, but even from the room where I wanted to be alone with her. I retained only Ki-Pai who, despite her surly airs and coarse remarks, revealed herself to be very devoted to her mistress and displayed great delicacy and tender skill in the care she took of her.

Clara's pulse still beat with the same reassuring regularity as though she had been in robust health. Life had not for a moment left this flesh which seemed for-ever dead. And both Ki-Pai and I were eager for her recovery. Suddenly she began to moan; the muscles of her face contracted, and light nervous spasms shook her throat, her arms and legs. Ki-Pai said:

"She will have a terrible crisis. You'll have to hold her firmly and take good care she doesn't claw her face and tear out her hair with her nails."

I thought she could hear me, and that, knowing me there beside her, the crisis Ki-Pai had predicted would be moderated. I murmured in her ear, attempting to put in my words all the caress of my voice, all the affection of my heart and also all the compassion—ah yes!—all the compassion in the world.

"Clara! Clara! It's I. Look at me... listen to me." But Ki-Pai stopped my mouth.

"Be quiet!" she said imperiously. "How can you expect her to hear us? She's still with the evil genii."

Then Clara began to struggle. All her muscles tightened, swelled and contracted frightfully... her articulations cracked, like the joints of a boat disabled in a storm. An expression of horrible suffering, all the more horrible for being silent, masked her face, contorted like the faces of the tortured men under the bell in the garden. Between her half-closed, twitching lids, only a slender bluish trace of her eyes showed. A little froth foamed at her lips. And, breathlessly, I groaned: "My God! my God! Is it possible? What's going to happen?" Ki-Pai commanded me:

"Hold her down... but leave her body free... for the demons must leave her body." And she added:

"It's the end. In a moment she will begin to cry."

We held her wrists, to prevent her from belaboring her face with her nails. And she had such strength I thought she would crush our hands. In a last convulsion her body was arched from her heels to her neck and taut skin quivered. Then, little by little the crisis abated. Her muscles relaxed, and she fell back exhausted on the bed, her eyes full of tears. For several moments she wept and wept. Tears flowed from her eyes, silently and ceaselessly, as from a spring!

"It's over," said Ki-Pai. "You may talk to her."

Her hand was now soft, moist, and burning in my own. Her eyes, still vague and distant, sought to recapture a consciousness of objects and shapes about her. She seemed to be returning from a long and agonizing sleep.

"Clara! my little Clara!" I murmured. For a long time she looked at me through her tears with a sad, hazy look.

"You," she said. "You... ah, yes." And her voice was like a whisper.

"It's I, it's I! Clara. Here I am. Do you recognize me?" She gave a sort of little hiccough, a little sob. And she stammered. "Oh, my darling! my darling! my poor darling!" Resting her head against mine, she begged me:

"Don't move. I'm all right like this... I'm pure like this... I'm all white... all white... like an anemone!"

I asked her if she was still suffering.

"No, no! I'm not suffering... and I'm happy to be here by you, quite little, beside you... quite little, quite little... and all white, white as those little swallows in the Chinese tales... you know... those little swallows."

With great difficulty, she uttered only little words... little words of purity and whiteness. On her lips there were only little flowers, little birds, little stars, little springs... and souls and wings, and heaven... heaven... heaven. Then, interrupting her babbling from time to time, she pressed my hand more strongly and rested, nestling her head against mine and saying more forcibly:

"Oh, my darling! never again, I swear to you! Never again, never again... never again!"

Ki-Pai had retired to the corner of the room, and in a low voice was singing a song, one of those songs which put little children to sleep and cradle them in their sleep.

"Never again... never again... never again!" repeated Clara, in a slow voice which was lost and melted into the slower and slower song Ki-Pai was singing. And she fell asleep against me, with a calm, clear, and deep sleep—deep as a great, gentle lake under a summer night's moon. Ki-Pai got up gently, noiselessly.

"I'm going," she said. "I'm going to sleep in the sampan. Tomorrow morning, when dawn comes, you will bring my mistress back to the palace. And it will begin all over again! It will always begin all over again!"

"Don't say that, Ki-Pai," I begged. "Just look at her sleeping against me, look at her sleeping so calm and pure a sleep, against me." The Chinese nodded her grimacing head, and with sad eyes, in which pity had replaced disgust, she murmured:

"I see her sleeping against you, and I tell you.—In eight days I'll accompany you both like this evening, on the river, coming from the Torture Garden. And after eight more years I'll accompany you the same way on the river, if you haven't gone away—and if I'm not dead!" She added:

"And if I am dead, some one else will accompany you with my mistress, on the river. And if you have gone away, some one else will accompany my mistress on the river. And nothing will be changed."

"Ki-Pai! Ki-Pai! Why do you say that? Look at her sleeping again. You don't know what you're saying!"

"Hush!" she said, placing her finger against her mouth. "Don't talk so loud. Don't move so much. Don't wake her up. At least, when she's asleep she can do no evil, either to others or herself." Walking carefully on tiptoe, like a nurse, she went to the door and opened it.

"Get out! Get out!" It was the voice of Ki-Pai, imperious among the buzzing voices of the women. And I could see nothing but painted eyes, painted faces, red mouths, tattooed breasts... and I heard the cries and the moans, the dances, sounds of flutes, the resonance of metal, and that name which ran and panted from mouth to mouth and shook the whole flower-boat like a spasm of love.

"Clara! Clara! Clara!"

The door closed, the noises were muffled, and the faces disappeared. And I was alone in the room where two lamps burned, draped with pink crepe... alone with Clara who was asleep and from time to time, repeated in her sleep, like a little dreaming child:

"Never again! Never again!"

And as though to belie those words, a bronze which I had not yet noticed, a fiercely sneering bronze ape crouching in the corner of the room extended towards Clara a monstrous phallus.

Ah, if only she might never awake!

"Clara! Clara! Clara!"

THE END

CPSIA information can be obtained
at www.ICGtesting.com
Printed in the USA
LVHW03s1609180918
590546LV00001B/130/P

9 781409 727682